Sarah Orne Jewett

A Native of Winby

And other tales

Sarah Orne Jewett

A Native of Winby
And other tales

ISBN/EAN: 9783337072315

Printed in Europe, USA, Canada, Australia, Japan

Cover: Foto ©Andreas Hilbeck / pixelio.de

More available books at **www.hansebooks.com**

A NATIVE OF WINBY

AND OTHER TALES

BY

SARAH ORNE JEWETT

BOSTON AND NEW YORK
HOUGHTON, MIFFLIN AND COMPANY
The Riverside Press, Cambridge
1898

CONTENTS.

A NATIVE OF WINBY.

I.

On the teacher's desk, in the little road-side school-house, there was a bunch of May-flowers, beside a dented and bent brass bell, a small Worcester's Dictionary without any cover, and a worn morocco-covered Bible. These were placed in an orderly row, and behind them was a small wooden box which held some broken pieces of blackboard crayon. The teacher, whom no timid new scholar could look at boldly, wore her accustomed air of authority and importance. She might have been nineteen years old,—not more,—but for the time being she scorned the frivolities of youth.

The hot May sun was shining in at the smoky small-paned windows; sometimes an outside shutter swung to with a creak, and eclipsed the glare. The narrow door stood wide open, to the left as you faced the desk, and an old spotted dog lay asleep on the step, and looked wise and old enough to have gone to school with several generations of children. It was half past three o'clock in the afternoon, and the primer class, settled into the apathy of after-recess fatigue, presented a straggling front, as they stood listlessly on the floor. As for the big boys and girls, they also were longing to be at liberty, but the pretty teacher, Miss Marilla Hender, seemed quite as energetic as when school was begun in the morning.

The spring breeze blew in at the open door, and even fluttered the primer leaves, but the back of the room felt hot and close, as if it were midsummer. The children in the class read their lessons in those high-keyed, droning voices which older teachers learn to associate with faint powers of perception. Only one or two of them had an awakened human look in their eyes, such as Matthew Arnold delighted himself in finding so often in the school-children of France. Most of these poor little students were as inadequate, at that weary moment, to the pursuit of letters as if they had been woolly spring lambs on a sunny hillside. The teacher corrected and admonished with great patience, glancing now and then toward points of danger and insurrection, whence came a suspicious buzz of whispering from behind a desk-lid or a pair of widespread large geographies. Now and then a toiling child would rise and come down the aisle, with his forefinger firm upon a puzzling word as if it were an unclassified insect. It was a lovely beckoning day out-of-doors. The children felt like captives; there was something that provoked rebellion in the droning voices, the buzzing of an early wild bee against the sunlit pane, and even in the stuffy familiar odor of the place, — the odor of apples and crumbs of doughnuts and gingerbread in the dinner pails on the high entry nails, and of all the little gowns and trousers that had brushed through junipers and young pines on their way to school.

The bee left his prisoning pane at last, and came over to the Mayflowers, which were in full bloom, although the season was very late, and deep in the woods there were still some graybacked snowdrifts, speckled with bits of bark and moss from the trees above.

"Come, come, Ezra!" urged the young teacher, rapping her desk sharply. "Stop watchin' that common bee! You know well enough what those letters spell. You won't learn to read at this rate until you are a grown man. Mind your book, now; you ought to remember who went to this school when he was a little boy. You 've heard folks tell about the Honorable Joseph K. Laneway? He used to be in primer just as you are now, and 't was n't long before he was out of it, either, and was called the smartest boy in school. He 's got to be a general and a Senator, and one of the richest men out West. You don't seem to have the least mite of ambition to-day, any of you!"

The exhortation, entirely personal in the beginning, had swiftly passed to a general rebuke. Ezra looked relieved, and the other children brightened up as they recognized a tale familiar to their ears. Anything was better than trying to study in that dull last hour of afternoon school.

"Yes," continued Miss Hender, pleased that she had at last roused something like proper attention, "you all ought to be proud that you are schoolmates of District Number Four, and can remember that the celebrated General Laneway had the same early advantages as you, and think what he has made of himself by perseverance and ambition."

The pupils were familiar enough with the illustrious history of their noble predecessor. They were sure to be told, in lawless moments, that if Mr. Laneway were to come in and see them he would be mortified to death; and the members of the school committee always referred to him, and said that he had been a poor boy, and was now a self-made man, — as if every man were not self-made as to his character and reputation!

At this point, young Johnny Spencer showed his next neighbor, in the back of his Colburn's Arithmetic, an imaginary portrait of their district hero, which caused them both to chuckle derisively. The Honorable Mr. Laneway figured on the flyleaf as an extremely cross-eyed person, with strangely crooked legs and arms and a terrific expression. He was outlined with red and blue pencils as to coat and trousers, and held a reddened scalp in one hand and a blue tomahawk in the other; being closely associated in the artist's mind with the early settlements of the far West.

There was a noise of wheels in the road near by, and, though Miss Hender had much more to say, everybody ceased to listen to her, and turned toward the windows, leaning far forward over their desks to see who might be passing. They caught a glimpse of a shiny carriage; the old dog bounded out, barking, but nothing passed the open door. The carriage had stopped; some one was coming to the school; somebody was going to be called out! It could not be the committee, whose pompous and uninspiring spring visit had taken place only the week before.

Presently a well-dressed elderly man, with an expectant, masterful look, stood on the doorstep, glanced in with a smile, and knocked. Miss Marilla Hender blushed, smoothed her pretty hair anxiously with both hands, and stepped down from her little platform to answer the summons. There was hardly a shut mouth in the primer class.

"Would it be convenient for you to receive a visitor to the school?" the stranger asked politely, with a fine bow of deference to Miss Hender. He looked much pleased and a little excited, and the teacher said, —

"Certainly; step right in, won't you, sir?" in quite another tone from that in which she had just addressed the school.

The boys and girls were sitting straight and silent in their places, in something like a fit of apprehension and unpreparedness at

such a great emergency. The guest repre-
sented a type of person previously unknown
in District Number Four. Everything about
him spoke of wealth and authority. The old
dog returned to the doorstep, and after a
careful look at the invader approached him,
with a funny doggish grin and a desperate
wag of the tail, to beg for recognition.

The teacher gave her chair on the platform
to the guest, and stood beside him with very
red cheeks, smoothing her hair again once or
twice, and keeping the hard-wood ruler fast
in hand, like a badge of office. "Primer
class may now retire!" she said firmly, although the lesson was not more than half
through; and the class promptly escaped to
their seats, waddling and stumbling, until
they all came up behind their desks, face
foremost, and added themselves to the number of staring young countenances. After
this there was a silence, which grew more and
more embarrassing.

"Perhaps you would be pleased to hear
our first class in geography, sir?" asked the
fair Marilla, recovering her presence of
mind; and the guest kindly assented.

The young teacher was by no means willing to give up a certainty for an uncertainty.

Yesterday's lesson had been well learned; she turned back to the questions about the State of Kansota, and at the first sentence the mysterious visitor's dignity melted into an unconscious smile. He listened intently for a minute, and then seemed to reoccupy himself with his own thoughts and purposes, looking eagerly about the old school-house, and sometimes gazing steadily at the children. The lesson went on finely, and when it was finished Miss Hender asked the girl at the head of the class to name the States and Territories, which she instantly did, mispronouncing nearly all the names of the latter; then others stated boundaries and capitals, and the resources of the New England States, passing on finally to the names of the Presidents. Miss Hender glowed with pride; she had worked hard over the geography class in the winter term, and it did not fail her on this great occasion. When she turned bravely to see if the gentleman would like to ask any questions, she found that he was apparently lost in a deep reverie, so she repeated her own question more distinctly.

"They have done very well, — very well indeed," he answered kindly; and then, to every one's surprise, he rose, went up the aisle, pushed Johnny Spencer gently along his bench, and sat down beside him. The space was cramped, and the stranger looked huge and uncomfortable, so that everybody laughed, except one of the big girls, who turned pale with fright, and thought he must be crazy. When this girl gave a faint squeak Miss Hender recovered herself, and rapped twice with the ruler to restore order; then became entirely tranquil. There had been talk of replacing the hacked and worn old school-desks with patent desks and chairs; this was probably an agent connected with that business. At once she was resolute and self-reliant, and said, " No whispering ! " in a firm tone that showed she did not mean to be trifled with. The geography class was dismissed, but the elderly gentleman, in his handsome overcoat, still sat there wedged in at Johnny Spencer's side.

" I presume, sir, that you are canvassing for new desks," said Miss Hender, with dignity. " You will have to see the supervisor and the selectmen." There did not seem to be any need of his lingering, but she had an ardent desire to be pleasing to a person of such evident distinction. " We always tell strangers — I thought, sir, you might be gratified to know — that this is the school-house where the Honorable Joseph K. Laneway first attended school. All do not know that he was born in this town, and went West very young; it is only about a mile from here where his folks used to live."

At this moment the visitor's eyes fell. He did not look at pretty Marilla any more, but opened Johnny Spencer's arithmetic, and, seeing the imaginary portrait of the great General Laneway, laughed a little, — a very deep-down comfortable laugh it was, — while Johnny himself turned cold with alarm, he could not have told why.

It was very still in the school-room; the bee was buzzing and bumping at the pane again; the moment was one of intense expectation.

The stranger looked at the children right and left. "The fact is this, young people," said he, in a tone that was half pride and half apology, "I am Joseph K. Laneway myself."

He tried to extricate himself from the narrow quarters of the desk, but for an embarrassing moment found that he was stuck fast. Johnny Spencer instinctively gave him an assisting push, and once free the great soldier, statesman, and millionaire took a few steps forward to the open floor; then, after hesitating a moment, he mounted the little platform and stood in the teacher's place. Marilla Hender was as pale as ashes.

"I have thought many times," the great guest began, "that some day I should come back to visit this place, which is so closely interwoven with the memories of my childhood. In my counting-room, on the fields of war, in the halls of Congress, and most of all in my Western home, my thoughts have flown back to the hills and brooks of Winby and to this little old school-house. I could shut ·my eyes and call back the buzz of voices, and fear my teacher's frown, and feel my boyish ambitions waking and stirring in my breast. On that bench where I just sat I saw some notches that I cut with my first jack-knife fifty-eight years ago this very spring. I remember the faces of the boys and girls who went to school with me, and I see their grandchildren before me. I know that one is a Goodsoe and another a Winn by the old family look. One generation goes, and another comes.

"There are many things that I might say to you. I meant, even in those early restricted days, to make my name known, and

I dare say that you too have ambition. Be careful what you wish for in this world, for if you wish hard enough you are sure to get it. I once heard a very wise man say this, and the longer I live the more firmly I believe it to be true. But wishing hard means working hard for what you want, and the world's prizes wait for the men and women who are ready to take pains to win them. Be careful and set your minds on the best things. I meant to be a rich man when I was a boy here, and I stand before you a rich man, knowing the care and anxiety and responsibility of wealth. I meant to go to Congress, and I am one of the Senators from Kansota. I say this as humbly as I say it proudly. I used to read of the valor and patriotism of the old Greeks and Romans with my youthful blood leaping along my veins, and it came to pass that my own country was in danger, and that I could help to fight her battles. Perhaps some one of these little lads has before him a more eventful life than I have lived, and is looking forward to activity and honor and the pride of fame. I wish him all the joy that I have had, all the toil that I have had, and all the bitter disappointments even; for adversity leads a man to depend upon that which is above him, and the path of glory is a lonely path, beset by temptations and a bitter sense of the weakness and imperfection of man. I see my life spread out like a great picture, as I stand here in my boyhood's place. I regret my failures. I thank God for what in his kind providence has been honest and right. I am glad to come back, but I feel, as I look in your young faces, that I am an old man, while your lives are just beginning. When you remember, in years to come, that I came here to see the old school-house, remember that I said: Wish for the best things, and work hard to win them ; try to be good men and women, for the honor of the school and the town, and the noble young country that gave you birth; be kind at home and generous abroad. Remember that I, an old man who had seen much of life, begged you to be brave and good."

The Honorable Mr. Laneway had rarely felt himself so moved in any of his public speeches, but he was obliged to notice that for once he could not hold his audience. The primer class especially had begun to flag in attention, but one or two faces among the elder scholars fairly shone with vital sympathy and a lovely prescience of their future. Their eyes met his as if they struck a flash of light. There was a sturdy boy who half rose in his place unconsciously, the color coming and going in his cheeks; something in Mr. Laneway's words lit the altar flame in his reverent heart.

Marilla Hender was pleased and a little dazed; she could not have repeated what her illustrious visitor had said, but she longed to tell everybody the news that he was in town, and had come to school to make an address. She had never seen a great man before, and really needed time to reflect upon him and to consider what she ought to say. She was just quivering with the attempt to make a proper reply and thank Mr. Laneway for the honor of his visit to the school, when he asked her which of the boys could be trusted to drive back his hired horse to the Four Corners. Eight boys, large and small, nearly every boy in the school, rose at once and snapped insistent fingers; but Johnny Spencer alone was desirous not to attract attention to himself. The Colburn's Intellectual Arithmetic with the portrait had been well secreted between his tight jacket and his shirt. Miss Hender selected a trustworthy freckled person in long trousers, who was half way to the door in an instant, and was heard almost immediately to shout loudly at the quiet horse.

Then the Hero of District Number Four made his acknowledgments to the teacher. "I fear that I have interrupted you too long," he said, with pleasing deference.

Marilla replied that it was of no consequence; she hoped he would call again. She may have spoken primly, but her pretty eyes said everything that her lips forgot. "My grandmother will want to see you, sir," she ventured to say. "I guess you will remember her, — Mis' Hender, she that was Abby Harran. She has often told me how you used to get your lessons out o' the same book."

"Abby Harran's granddaughter?" Mr. Laneway looked at her again with fresh interest. "Yes, I wish to see her more than any one else. Tell her that I am coming to see her before I go away, and give her my love. Thank you, my dear," as Marilla offered his missing hat. "Good-by, boys and girls." He stopped and looked at them once more from the boys' entry, and turned again to look back from the very doorstep.

"Good-by, sir, — good-by," piped two or three of the young voices; but most of the children only stared, and neither spoke nor moved.

"We will omit the class in Fourth Reader this afternoon. The class in grammar may recite," said Miss Hender in her most contained and official manner.

The grammar class sighed like a single pupil, and obeyed. She was very stern with the grammar class, but every one in school had an inner sense that it was a great day in the history of District Number Four.

II.

The Honorable Mr. Laneway found the outdoor air very fresh and sweet after the closeness of the school-house. It had just that same odor in his boyhood, and as he escaped he had a delightful sense of playing truant or of having an unexpected holiday. It was easier to think of himself as a boy, and to slip back into boyish thoughts, than to bear the familiar burden of his manhood. He climbed the tumble-down stone wall across the road, and went along a narrow path to the spring that bubbled up clear and cold under a great red oak. How many times he had longed for a drink of that water, and now here it was, and the thirst of that warm spring day was hard to quench! Again and again he stopped to fill the birch-bark dipper which the school-children had made, just as his own comrades made theirs years before. The oak-tree was dying at the top. The pine woods beyond had been cut and had grown again since his boyhood, and looked much as he remembered them. Beyond the spring and away from the woods the path led across overgrown pastures to another road, perhaps three quarters of a mile away, and near this road was the small farm which had been his former home. As he walked slowly along, he was met again and again by some reminder of his youthful days. He had always liked to refer to his early life in New England in his political addresses, and had spoken more than once of going to find the cows at nightfall in the autumn evenings, and being glad to warm his bare feet in the places where the sleepy beasts had lain, before he followed their slow steps homeward through bush and brier. The Honorable Mr. Laneway had a touch of true sentiment which added much to his really stirring and effective campaign speeches. He had often been called the "king of the platform" in his adopted State. He had long ago grown used to saying "Go" to one man, and "Come" to another, like the ruler of old; but all his natural power of leadership and habit of authority disappeared at once as he trod the pasture slopes, calling back the remembrance of his childhood. Here was the place where two lads, older than himself, had killed a terrible woodchuck at bay in the angle of a great rock; and just beyond was the sunny spot where he had picked a bunch of pink and white anemones under a prickly barberry thicket, to give to Abby Harran in morning school. She had put them into her desk, and let them wilt there, but she was pleased when she took them. Abby Harran, the little teacher's grandmother, was a year older than he, and had wakened the earliest thought of love in his youthful breast.

It was almost time to catch the first sight of his birthplace. From the knoll just ahead he had often seen the light of his mother's lamp, as he came home from school on winter afternoons; but when he reached the knoll the old house was gone, and so was the great walnut - tree that grew beside it, and a pang of disappointment shot through this devout pilgrim's heart. He never had doubted that the old farm was somebody's home still, and had counted upon the pleasure of spending a night there, and sleeping again in that room under the roof, where the rain sounded loud, and the walnut branches brushed to and fro when the wind blew, as if they were the claws of tigers. He hurried across the worn-out fields, long ago turned into sheep pastures, where the last year's tall grass and golden-rod stood gray and winter-killed; tracing the old walls and fences, and astonished to see how small the fields had been. The prosperous owner of Western farming lands could not help remembering those widespread luxuriant acres, and the broad outlooks of his Western home.

It was difficult at first to find exactly where the house had stood; even the foundations had disappeared. At last in the long, faded grass he discovered the doorstep, and near by was a little mound where the great walnut-tree stump had been. The cellar was a mere dent in the sloping ground; it had been filled in by the growing grass and slow processes of summer and winter weather.

But just at the pilgrim's right were some
thorny twigs of an old rosebush. A sudden
brightening of memory brought to mind the
love that his mother — dead since his fif-
teenth year — had kept for this sweetbrier.
How often she had wished that she had
brought it to her new home! So much had
changed in the world, so many had gone into
the world of light, and here the faithful
blooming thing was yet alive! There was
one slender branch where green buds were
starting, and getting ready to flower in the
new year.

The afternoon wore late, and still the gray-
haired man lingered. He might have laughed
at some one else who gave himself up to sad
thoughts, and found fault with himself, with
no defendant to plead his cause at the bar of
conscience. It was an altogether lonely hour.
He had dreamed all his life, in a sentimental,
self-satisfied fashion, of this return to Winby.
It had always appeared to be a grand affair,
but so far he was himself the only interested
spectator at his poor occasion. There was
even a dismal consciousness that he had been
undignified, perhaps even a little consequen-
tial and silly, in the old school-house. The
picture of himself on the war-path, in Johnny

Spencer's arithmetic, was the only tribute that this longed-for day had held, but he laughed aloud delightedly at the remembrance and really liked that solemn little boy who sat at his own old desk. There was another older lad, who sat at the back of the room, who reminded Mr. Laneway of himself in his eager youth. There was a spark of light in that fellow's eyes. Once or twice in the earlier afternoon, as he drove along, he had asked people in the road if there were a Laneway family in that neighborhood, but everybody had said no in indifferent fashion. Somehow he had been expecting that every one would know him and greet him, and give him credit for what he had tried to do, but old Winby had her own affairs to look after, and did very well without any of his help.

Mr. Laneway acknowledged to himself at this point that he was weak and unmanly. There must be some old friends who would remember him, and give him as hearty a welcome as the greeting he had brought for them. So he rose and went his way westward toward the sunset. The air was growing damp and cold, and it was time to make sure of shelter. This was hardly like the visit he had meant to pay to his birthplace.

He wished with all his heart that he had never come back. But he walked briskly away, intent upon wider thoughts as the fresh evening breeze quickened his steps. He did not consider where he was going, but was for a time the busy man of affairs, stimulated by the unconscious influence of his surroundings. The slender gray birches and pitch pines of that neglected pasture had never before seen a hat and coat exactly in the fashion. They may have been abashed by the presence of a United States Senator and Western millionaire, though a piece of New England ground that had often felt the tread of his bare feet was not likely to quake because a pair of smart shoes stepped hastily along the school-house path.

III.

There was an imperative knock at the side door of the Hender farmhouse, just after dark. The young school-mistress had come home late, because she had stopped all the way along to give people the news of her afternoon's experience. Marilla was not coy and speechless any longer, but sat by the kitchen stove telling her eager grandmother everything she could remember or could imagine.

"Who 's that knocking at the door?" interrupted Mrs. Hender. "No, I 'll go myself; I 'm nearest."

The man outside was cold and foot-weary. He was not used to spending a whole day unrecognized, and, after being first amused, and even enjoying a sense of freedom at escaping his just dues of consideration and respect, he had begun to feel as if he were old and forgotten, and was hardly sure of a friend in the world.

Old Mrs. Hender came to the door, with her eyes shining with delight, in great haste to dismiss whoever had knocked, so that she might hear the rest of Marilla's story. She opened the door wide to whoever might have come on some country errand, and looked the tired and faint-hearted Mr. Laneway full in the face.

"Dear heart, come in!" she exclaimed, reaching out and taking him by the shoulder, as he stood humbly on a lower step. "Come right in, Joe. Why, I should know you anywhere! Why, Joe Laneway, *you same boy!*"

In they went to the warm, bright, country kitchen. The delight and kindness of an old friend's welcome and her instant sympathy seemed the loveliest thing in the world. They sat down in two old straight-backed kitchen chairs. They still held each other by the hand, and looked in each other's face. The plain old room was aglow with heat and cheerfulness; the tea-kettle was singing; a drowsy cat sat on the wood-box with her paws tucked in; and the house dog came forward in a friendly way, wagging his tail, and laid his head on their clasped hands.

"And to think I have n't seen you since your folks moved out West, the next spring after you were thirteen in the winter," said the good woman. "But I s'pose there ain't been anybody that has followed your career closer than I have, accordin' to their opportunities. You 've done a great work for your country, Joe. I 'm proud of you clean through. Sometimes folks has said, 'There, there, Mis' Hender, what be you goin' to say now?' but I 've always told 'em to wait. I knew you saw your reasons. You was always an honest boy." The tears started and shone in her kind eyes. Her face showed that she had waged a bitter war with poverty and sorrow, but the look of affection that it wore, and the warm touch of her hard hand, misshapen and worn with toil, touched her old friend in his inmost heart, and for a minute neither could speak.

"They do say that women folks have got no natural head for politics, but I always could seem to sense what was goin' on in Washington, if there was any sense to it," said grandmother Hender at last.

"Nobody could puzzle you at school, I remember," answered Mr. Laneway, and they both laughed heartily. "But surely this granddaughter does not make your household? You have sons?"

"Two beside her father. He died; but they 're both away, up toward Canada, buying cattle. We are getting along considerable well these last few years, since they got a mite o' capital together; but the old farm was n't really able to maintain us, with the heavy expenses that fell on us unexpected year by year. I 've seen a great sight of trouble, Joe. My boy John, Marilla's father, and his nice wife, — I lost 'em both early, when Marilla was but a child. John was the flower o' my family. He would have made a name for himself. You would have taken to John."

"I was sorry to hear of your loss," said Mr. Laneway. "He was a brave man. I know what he did at Fredericksburg. You remember that I lost my wife and my only son?"

There was a silence between the friends, who had no need for words now; they understood each other's heart only too well. Marilla, who sat near them, rose and went out of the room.

"Yes, yes, daughter," said Mrs. Hender, calling her back, "we ought to be thinkin' about supper."

"I was going to light a little fire in the parlor," explained Marilla, with a slight tone of rebuke in her clear girlish voice.

"Oh, no, you ain't, — not now, at least," protested the elder woman decidedly. "Now, Joseph, what should you like to have for supper? I wish to my heart I had some fried turnovers, like those you used to come after when you was a boy. I can make 'em just about the same as mother did. I 'll be bound you 've thought of some old-fashioned dish that you 'd relish for your supper."

"Rye drop-cakes, then, if they would n't give you too much trouble," answered the Honorable Joseph, with prompt seriousness, "and don't forget some cheese." He looked up at his old playfellow as she stood beside him, eager with affectionate hospitality.

"You 've no idea what a comfort Marilla 's been," she stooped to whisper. "Always took right hold and helped me when she was a baby. She 's as good as made up already to me for my having no daughter. I want you to get acquainted with Marilla."

The granddaughter was still awed and anxious about the entertainment of so distinguished a guest when her grandmother appeared at last in the pantry.

"I ain't goin' to let you do no such a thing, darlin'," said Abby Hender, when Marilla spoke of making something that she called "fairy gems" for tea, after a new and essentially feminine recipe. "You just let me get supper to-night. The Gen'ral has enough kickshaws to eat; he wants a good, hearty, old-fashioned supper, — the same country cooking he remembers when he was a boy. He went so far himself as to speak of rye drop-cakes, an' there ain't one in a hundred, nowadays, knows how to make the kind he means. You go an' lay the table just as we always have it, except you can get out them old big sprigged cups o' my mother's. Don't put on none o' the parlor cluset things."

Marilla went off crestfallen and demurring. She had a noble desire to show Mr. Laneway that they knew how to have things as well as anybody, and was sure that he would consider it more polite to be asked into the best room, and to sit there alone until tea was ready; but the illustrious Mr. Laneway was allowed to stay in the kitchen, in apparent happiness, and to watch the proceedings from beginning to end. The two old friends talked industriously, but he saw his rye drop-cakes go into the oven and come out, and his tea made, and his piece of salt fish broiled and buttered, a broad piece of honeycomb set on to match some delightful thick slices of brown-crusted loaf bread, and all the simple feast prepared. There was a sufficient piece of Abby Hender's best cheese; it must be confessed that there were also some baked beans, and, as one thing after another appeared, the Honorable Joseph K. Laneway grew hungrier and hungrier, until he fairly looked pale with anticipation and delay, and was bidden at that very moment to draw up his chair and make himself a supper if he could.

What cups of tea, what uncounted rye drop-cakes, went to the making of that successful supper! How gay the two old friends became, and of what old stories they reminded each other, and how late the dark spring evening grew, before the feast was over and the straight-backed chairs were set against the kitchen wall!

Marilla listened for a time with more or less interest, but at last she took one of her school-books, with slight ostentation, and went over to study by the lamp. Mrs. Hender had brought her knitting-work, a blue woolen stocking, out of a drawer, and sat down serene and unruffled, prepared to keep awake as late as possible. She was a woman who had kept her youthful looks through the difficulties of farm life as few women can, and this added to her guest's sense of home-likeness and pleasure. There was something that he felt to be sisterly and comfortable in her strong figure; he even noticed the little plaid woolen shawl that she wore about her shoulders. Dear, uncomplaining heart of Abby Hender! The appealing friendliness of the good woman made no demands except to be allowed to help and to serve everybody who came in her way.

Now began in good earnest the talk of old times, and what had become of this and that old schoolmate; how one family had come to want and another to wealth. The changes and losses and windfalls of good fortune in that rural neighborhood were made tragedy and comedy by turns in Abby Hender's dramatic speech. She grew younger and more entertaining hour by hour, and beguiled the grave Senator into confidential talk of national affairs. He had much to say, to which she listened with rare sympathy and intelligence. She astonished him by her comprehension of difficult questions of the day, and by her simple good sense. Marilla grew hopelessly sleepy, and departed, but neither of them turned to notice her as she lingered a moment at the door to say good-night. When the immediate subjects of conversation were fully discussed, however, there was an unexpected interval of silence, and, after making sure that her knitting stitches counted exactly right, Abby Hender cast a questioning glance at the Senator to see if he had it in mind to go to bed. She was reluctant to end her evening so soon, but determined to act the part of considerate hostess. The guest was as wide awake as ever: eleven o'clock was the best part of his evening.

"Cider?" he suggested, with an expectant smile, and Abby Hender was on her feet in a moment. When she had brought a pitcher from the pantry, he took a candle from the high shelf and led the way.

"To think of your remembering our old cellar candlestick all these years!" laughed the pleased woman, as she followed him down the steep stairway, and then laughed still more at his delight in the familiar look of the place.

"Unchanged as the pyramids!" he said. "I suppose those pound sweetings that used to be in that farthest bin were eaten up months ago?"

It was plain to see that the household stores were waning low, as befitted the time of year, but there was still enough in the old cellar. Care and thrift and gratitude made the poor farmhouse a rich place. This woman of real ability had spent her strength from youth to age, and had lavished as much industry and power of organization in her narrow sphere as would have made her famous in a wider one. Joseph Laneway could not help sighing as he thought of it.

How many things this good friend had missed, and yet how much she had been able to win that makes everywhere the very best of life! Poor and early widowed, there must have been a constant battle with poverty on that stony Harran farm, whose owners had been pitied even in his early boyhood, when the best of farming life was none too easy. But Abby Hender had always been one of the leaders of the town.

"Now, before we sit down again, I want you to step into my best room. Perhaps you won't have time in the morning, and I 've got something to show you," she said persuasively.

It was a plain, old-fashioned best room, with a look of pleasantness in spite of the spring chill and the stiffness of the best chairs. They lingered before the picture of Mrs. Hender's soldier son, a poor work of a poorer artist in crayons, but the spirit of the young face shone out appealingly. Then they crossed the room and stood before some bookshelves, and Abby Hender's face brightened into a beaming smile of triumph.

"You did n't expect we should have all those books, now, did you, Joe Laneway?" she asked.

He shook his head soberly, and leaned forward to read the titles. There were no very new ones, as if times had been hard of late; almost every volume was either history, or biography, or travel. Their owner had reached out of her own narrow boundaries into other lives and into far countries. He recognized with gratitude two or three congressional books that he had sent her when he first went to Washington, and there was a life of himself, written from a partisan point of view, and issued in one of his most exciting campaigns; the sight of it touched him to the heart, and then she opened it, and showed him the three or four letters that he had written her, — one, in boyish handwriting, describing his adventures on his first Western journey.

"There are a hundred and six volumes now," announced the proud owner of such a library. "I lend 'em all I can, or most of them would look better. I have had to wait a good while for some, and some were n't what I expected 'em to be, but most of 'em 's as good books as there is in the world. I 've never been so situated that it seemed best for me to indulge in a daily paper, and I don't know but it 's just as well; but stories were

never any great of a temptation. I know
pretty well what's goin' on about me, and I
can make that do. Real life's interestin'
enough for me."

Mr. Laneway was still looking over the
books. His heart smote him for not being
thoughtful; he knew well enough that the
overflow of his own library would have been
delightful to this self-denying, eager-minded
soul. "I've been a very busy man all my
life, Abby," he said impulsively, as if she
waited for some apology for his forgetful-
ness, "but I'll see to it now that you have
what you want to read. I don't mean to
lose hold of your advice on state matters."
They both laughed, and he added, "I've always thought of you, if I haven't shown it."

"There's more time to read than there
used to be; I've had what was best for me,"
answered the woman gently, with a grateful
look on her face, as she turned to glance at
her old friend. "Marilla takes hold wonder-
fully and helps me with the work. In the
long winter evenings you can't think what
a treat a new book is. I wouldn't change
places with the queen."

They had come back to the kitchen, and
she stood before the cupboard, reaching high

for two old gayly striped crockery mugs. There were some doughnuts and cheese at hand; their early supper seemed quite forgotten. The kitchen was warm, and they had talked themselves thirsty and hungry; but with what an unexpected tang the cider freshened their throats! Mrs. Hender had picked the apples herself that went to the press; they were all chosen from the old russet tree and the gnarly, red-cheeked, ungrafted fruit that grew along the lane. The flavor made one think of frosty autumn mornings on high hillsides, of north winds and sunny skies. "It 'livens one to the heart," as Mrs. Hender remarked proudly, when the Senator tried to praise it as much as it deserved, and finally gave a cheerful laugh, such as he had not laughed for many a day.

"Why, it seems like drinking the month of October," he told her; and at this the hostess reached over, protesting that the striped mug was too narrow to hold what it ought, and filled it up again.

"Oh, Joe Laneway, to think that I see you at last, after all these years!" she said. "How rich I shall feel with this evening to live over! I 've always wanted to see somebody that I 'd read about, and now I 've got

that to remember; but I 've always known I
should see you again, and I believe 't was
the Lord's will."

Early the next morning they said good-by.
The early breakfast had to be hurried, and
Marilla was to drive Mr. Laneway to the station, three miles away. It was Saturday
morning, and she was free from school.

Mr. Laneway strolled down the lane before breakfast was ready, and came back with
a little bunch of pink anemones in his hand.
Marilla thought that he meant to give them
to her, but he laid them beside her grandmother's plate. "You must n't put those in
your desk," he said with a smile, and Abby
Hender blushed like a girl.

"I 've got those others now, dried and put
away somewhere in one of my books," she
said quietly, and Marilla wondered what they
meant.

The two old friends shook hands warmly
at parting. "I wish you could have stayed
another day, so I could have had the minister
come and see you," urged Mrs. Hender regretfully.

"You could n't have done any more for
me. I have had the best visit in the world,"

he answered, a little shaken, and holding her hand a moment longer, while Marilla sat, young and impatient, in the high wagon. "You're a dear good woman, Abby. Sometimes when things have gone wrong I've been sorry that I ever had to leave Winby."

The woman's clear eyes looked straight into his; then fell. "You wouldn't have done everything you have for the country," she said.

"Give me a kiss; we're getting to be old folks now," said the General; and they kissed each other gravely.

A moment later Abby Hender stood alone in her dooryard, watching and waving her hand again and again, while the wagon rattled away down the lane and turned into the highroad.

Two hours after Marilla returned from the station, and rushed into the kitchen.

"Grandma!" she exclaimed, "you never did see such a crowd in Winby as there was at the depot! Everybody in town had got word about General Laneway, and they were pushing up to shake hands, and cheering same as at election, and the cars waited much as ten minutes, and all the folks was lookin' out of the windows, and came out on the platforms when they heard who it was. Folks say that he 'd been to see the selectmen yesterday before he came to school, and he 's goin' to build an elegant town hall, and have the names put up in it of all the Winby men that went to the war." Marilla sank into a chair, flushed with excitement. "Everybody was asking me about his being here last night and what he said to the school. I wished that you 'd gone down to the depot instead of me."

"I had the best part of anybody," said Mrs. Hender, smiling and going on with her Saturday morning work. "I 'm real glad they showed him proper respect," she added a moment afterward, but her voice faltered.

"Why, you ain't been cryin', grandma?" asked the girl. "I guess you 're tired. You had a real good time, now, did n't you?"

"Yes, dear heart!" said Abby Hender. "'T ain't pleasant to be growin' old, that 's all. I could n't help noticin' his age as he rode away. I 've always been lookin' forward to seein' him again, an' now it 's all over."

DECORATION DAY.

I.

A WEEK before the thirtieth of May, three friends — John Stover and Henry Merrill and Asa Brown — happened to meet on Saturday evening at Barton's store at the Plains. They were ready to enjoy this idle hour after a busy week. After long easterly rains, the sun had at last come out bright and clear, and all the Barlow farmers had been planting. There was even a good deal of ploughing left to be done, the season was so backward.

The three middle-aged men were old friends. They had been school-fellows, and when they were hardly out of their boyhood the war came on, and they enlisted in the same company, on the same day, and happened to march away elbow to elbow. Then came the great experience of a great war, and the years that followed their return from the South had come to each almost alike.

These men might have been members of the same rustic household, they knew each other's history so well.

They were sitting on a low wooden bench at the left of the store door as you went in. People were coming and going on their Saturday night errands, — the post-office was in Barton's store, — but the friends talked on eagerly, without being interrupted, except by an occasional nod of recognition. They appeared to take no notice at all of the neighbors whom they saw oftenest. It was a most beautiful evening; the two great elms were almost half in leaf over the blacksmith's shop which stood across the wide road. Farther along were two small old-fashioned houses and the old white church, with its pretty belfry of four arched sides and a tiny dome at the top. The large cockerel on the vane was pointing a little south of west, and there was still light enough to make it shine bravely against the deep blue eastern sky. On the western side of the road, near the store, were the parsonage and the storekeeper's modern house, which had a French roof and some attempt at decoration, which the long-established Barlow people called gingerbread-work, and regarded with mingled pride and disdain. These buildings made the tiny village called Barlow Plains. They stood in the middle of a long narrow strip of level ground. They were islanded by green fields and pastures. There were hills beyond; the mountains themselves seemed very near. Scattered about on the hill slopes were farmhouses, which stood so far apart, with their clusters of out-buildings, that each looked lonely, and the pine woods above seemed to besiege them all. It was lighter on the uplands than it was in the valley, where the three men sat on their bench, with their backs to the store and the western sky.

"Well, here we be 'most into June, an' I 'ain't got a bush-bean above ground," lamented Henry Merrill.

"Your land 's always late, ain't it? But you always catch up with the rest on us," Asa Brown consoled him. "I 've often observed that your land, though early planted, was late to sprout. I view it there 's a good week's difference betwixt me an' Stover an' your folks, but come first o' July we all even up."

"'T is just so," said John Stover, taking his pipe out of his mouth, as if he had a good deal more to say, and then replacing it, as if he had changed his mind.

"Made it extry hard having that long wet spell. Can't none on us take no day off this season," said Asa Brown; but nobody thought it worth his while to respond to such evident truth.

"Next Saturday 'll be the thirtieth o' May — that 's Decoration Day, ain't it? — come round again. Lord! how the years slip by after you git to be forty-five an' along there!" said Asa again. "I s'pose some o' our folks 'll go over to Alton to see the procession, same 's usual. I 've got to git one o' them small flags to stick on our Joel's grave, an' Mis' Dexter always counts on havin' some for Harrison's lot. I calculate to get 'em somehow. I must make time to ride over, but I don't know where the time 's comin' from out o' next week. I wish the women folks would tend to them things. There 's the spot where Eb Munson an' John Tighe lays in the poor-farm lot, an' I did mean certain to buy flags for 'em last year an' year before, but I went an' forgot it. I 'd like to have folks that rode by notice 'em for once, if they was town paupers. Eb Munson was as darin' a man as ever stepped out to tuck o' drum."

"So he was," said John Stover, taking his pipe with decision and knocking out the ashes. "Drink was his ruin; but I wan't one that could be harsh with Eb, no matter what he done. He worked hard long's he could, too; but he wan't like a sound man, an' I think he took somethin' first not so much 'cause he loved it, but to kind of keep his strength up so's he could work, an' then, all of a sudden, rum clinched with him an' threw him. Eb was talkin' 'long o' me one day when he was about half full, an' says he, right out, 'I would n't have fell to this state,' says he, 'if I'd had me a home an' a little fam'ly; but it don't make no difference to nobody, and it's the best comfort I seem to have, an' I ain't goin' to do without it. I'm ailin' all the time,' says he, 'an' if I keep middlin' full, I make out to hold my own an' to keep along o' my work.' I pitied Eb. I says to him, 'You ain't goin' to bring no disgrace on us old army boys, be you, Eb?' an' he says no, he wan't. I think if he'd lived to get one o' them big fat pensions, he'd had it easier. Eight dollars a month paid his board, while he'd pick up what cheap work he could, an' then he got so that decent folks did n't seem to want the bother of him, an' so he come on the town."

"There was somethin' else to it," said Henry Merrill soberly. "Drink come natural to him, 't was born in him, I expect, an' there wan't nobody that could turn the divil out same 's they did in Scriptur'. His father an' his gran'father was drinkin' men; but they was kind-hearted an' good neighbors, an' never set out to wrong nobody. 'T was the custom to drink in their day; folks was colder an' lived poorer in early times, an' that's how most of 'em kept a-goin'. But what stove Eb all up was his disapp'intment with Marthy Peck — her forsakin' of him an' marryin' old John Down whilst Eb was off to war. I 've always laid it up ag'inst her."

"So 've I," said Asa Brown. "She did n't use the poor fellow right. I guess she was full as well off, but it 's one thing to show judgment, an' another thing to have heart."

There was a long pause; the subject was too familiar to need further comment.

"There ain't no public sperit here in Barlow," announced Asa Brown, with decision. "I don't s'pose we could ever get up anything for Decoration Day. I 've felt kind of 'shamed, but it always comes in a busy time; 't wan't no time to have it, anyway, right in late plantin'."

"'T ain't no use to look for public sperit 'less you've got some yourself," observed John Stover soberly; but something had pleased him in the discouraged suggestion. "Perhaps we could mark the day this year. It comes on a Saturday; that ain't nigh so bad as bein' in the middle of the week."

Nobody made any answer, and presently he went on, —

"There was a time along back when folks was too nigh the war-time to give much thought to the bigness of it. The best fellows was them that had stayed to home an' worked their trades an' laid up money; but I don't know 's it's so now."

"Yes, the fellows that stayed at home got all the fat places, an' when we come back we felt dreadful behind the times," grumbled Asa Brown. "I remember how 't was."

"They begun to call us heroes an' old stick-in-the-mud just about the same time," resumed Stover, with a chuckle. "We wa'n't no hand for strippin' woodland nor even tradin' hosses them first few years. I don' know why 't was we were so beat out. The best most on us could do was to sag right on to the old folks. Father he never wanted me to go to the war, — 't was partly his Quaker breed, — an' he used to be dreadful mortified with the way I hung round down here to the store an' loafed round a-talkin' about when I was out South, an' arguin' with folks that did n't know nothin', about what the generals done. There! I see me now just as he see me then; but after I had my boy-strut out, I took holt o' the old farm 'long o' father, an' I 've made it bounce. Look at them old meadows an' see the herd's grass that come off of 'em last year! I ain't ashamed o' my place now, if I did go to the war."

"It all looks a sight bigger to me now than it did then," said Henry Merrill. "Our goin' to the war, I refer to. We did n't sense it no more than other folks did. I used to be sick o' hearin' their stuff about patriotism and lovin' your country, an' them pieces o' poetry women folks wrote for the papers on the old flag, an' our fallen heroes, an' them things; they did n't seem to strike me in the right place; but I tell ye it kind o' starts me now every time I come on the flag sud-den, — it does so. A spell ago — 'long in the fall, I guess it was — I was over to Al-ton, an' there was a fire company paradin'. They 'd got the prize at a fair, an' had just

come home on the cars, an' I heard the band;
so I stepped to the front o' the store where
me an' my woman was tradin', an' the company felt well, an' was comin' along the street
'most as good as troops. I see the old flag
a-comin', kind of blowin' back, an' it went
all over me. Somethin' worked round in my
throat; I vow I come near cryin'. I was
glad nobody see me."

"I 'd go to war again in a minute," declared Stover, after an expressive pause;
"but I expect we should know better what
we was about. I don' know but we 've got
too many rooted opinions now to make us
the best o' soldiers."

"Martin Tighe an' John Tighe was considerable older than the rest, and they
done well," answered Henry Merrill quickly.
"We three was the youngest of any, but we
did think at the time we knew the most."

"Well, whatever you may say, that war
give the country a great start," said Asa
Brown. "I tell ye we just begin to see the
scope on 't. There was my cousin, you know,
Dan'l Evins, that stopped with us last winter; he was tellin' me that one o' his coastin'
trips he was into the port o' Beaufort lo'din'
with yaller-pine lumber, an' he roved into an

old buryin'-ground there is there, an' he see a stone that had on it some young Southern fellow's name that was killed in the war, an' under it was, 'He died for his country.' Dan'l knowed how I used to feel about them South Car'lina goings on, an' I did feel kind o' red an' ugly for a minute, an' then somethin' come over me, an' I says, 'Well, I don' know but what the poor chap did, Dan Evins, when you come to view it all round.'"

The other men made no answer.

"Le's see what we can do this year. I don't care if we be a poor han'ful," urged Henry Merrill. "The young folks ought to have the good of it; I'd like to have my boys see somethin' different. Le's get together what men there is. How many's left, anyhow? I know there was thirty-seven went from old Barlow, three-months' men an' all."

"There can't be over eight now, countin' out Martin Tighe; he can't march," said Stover. "No, 't ain't worth while." But the others did not notice his disapproval.

"There's nine in all," announced Asa Brown, after pondering and counting two or three times on his fingers. "I can't make us no more. I never could carry figur's in my head."

"I make nine," said Merrill. "We'll have Martin ride, an' Jesse Dean too, if he will. He's awful lively on them canes o' his. An' there's Jo Wade with his crutch; he's amazin' spry for a short distance. But we can't let 'em go far afoot; they're decripped men. We'll make 'em all put on what they've got left o' their uniforms, an' we'll scratch round an' have us a fife an' drum, an' make the best show we can."

"Why, Martin Tighe's boy, the next to the oldest, is an excellent hand to play the fife!" said John Stover, suddenly growing enthusiastic. "If you two are set on it, let's have a word with the minister to-morrow, an' see what he says. Perhaps he'll give out some kind of a notice. You have to have a good many bunches o' flowers. I guess we'd better call a meetin', some few on us, an' talk it over first o' the week. 'T wouldn't be no great of a range for us to take to march from the old buryin'-ground at the meetin'-house here up to the poor-farm an' round by Deacon Elwell's lane, so 's to notice them two stones he set up for his boys that was sunk on the man-o'-war. I expect they notice stones same 's if the folks laid there, don't they?"

He spoke wistfully. The others knew that Stover was thinking of the stone he had set up to the memory of his only brother, whose nameless grave had been made somewhere in the Wilderness.

"I don't know but what they'll be mad if we don't go by every house in town," he added anxiously, as they rose to go home. "'T is a terrible scattered population in Barlow to favor with a procession."

It was a mild starlit night. The three friends took their separate ways presently, leaving the Plains road and crossing the fields by foot-paths toward their farms.

II.

The week went by, and the next Saturday morning brought fair weather. It was a busy morning on the farms — like any other; but long before noon the teams of horses and oxen were seen going home from work in the fields, and everybody got ready in haste for the great event of the afternoon. It was so seldom that any occasion roused public interest in Barlow that there was an unexpected response, and the green before the old white meeting-house was covered with country wagons and groups of people, whole families together, who had come on foot. The old soldiers were to meet in the church; at half past .one the procession was to start, and on its return the minister was to make an address in the old burying-ground. John Stover had been first lieutenant in the war, so he was made captain of the day. A man from the next town had offered to drum for them, and Martin Tighe's proud boy was present with his fife. He had a great longing — strange enough in that peaceful, sheep-raising neighborhood — to go into the army; but he and his elder brother were the mainstay of their crippled father, and he could not be spared from the large household until a younger brother could take his place; so that all his fire and military zeal went for the present into martial tunes, and the fife was a safety-valve for his enthusiasm.

The army men were used to seeing each other; everybody knew everybody in the little country town of Barlow; but when one comrade after another appeared in what remained of his accoutrements, they felt the day to be greater than they had planned, and the simple ceremony proved more solemn than

any one expected. They could make no use
of their every-day jokes and friendly greet-
ings. Their old blue coats and tarnished
army caps looked faded and antiquated
enough. One of the men had nothing left
but his rusty canteen and rifle; but these he
carried like sacred emblems. He had worn
out all his army clothes long ago, because
he was too poor when he was discharged to
buy any others.

When the door of the church opened, the
veterans were not abashed by the size and
silence of the crowd. They came walking
two by two down the steps, and took their
places in line as if there were nobody looking
on. Their brief evolutions were like a mystic
rite. The two lame men refused to do anything but march as best they could; but poor
Martin Tighe, more disabled than they, was
brought out and lifted into Henry Merrill's
best wagon, where he sat up, straight and
soldierly, with his boy for driver. There was
a little flag in the whip-socket before him,
which flapped gayly in the breeze. It was
such a long time since he had been seen out-
of-doors that everybody found him a great
object of interest, and paid him much attention. Even those who were tired of being

asked to contribute to his support, who resented the fact of his having a helpless wife and great family; who always insisted that with his little pension and hopeless lameness, his fingerless left hand and failing sight, he could support himself and his household if he chose, — even those persons came forward now to greet him handsomely and with large approval. To be sure, he enjoyed the conversation of idlers, and his wife had a complaining way that was the same as begging, especially since her boys began to grow up and be of some use; and there were one or two near neighbors who never let them really want; so other people, who had cares enough of their own, could excuse themselves for forgetting him the year round, and even call him shiftless. But there were none to look askance at Martin Tighe on Decoration Day, as he sat in the wagon, with his bleached face like a captive's, and his thin, afflicted body. He stretched out his whole hand impartially to those who had remembered and those who had forgotten both his courage at Fredericksburg and his sorry need in Barlow.

Henry Merrill had secured the engine company's large flag in Alton, and now carried it proudly. There were eight men in line, two by two, and marching a good bit apart, to make their line the longer. The fife and drum struck up gallantly together, and the little procession moved away slowly along the country road. It gave an unwonted touch of color to the landscape, — the scarlet, the blue, between the new-ploughed fields and budding roadside thickets, between the wide dim ranges of the mountains, under the great white clouds of the spring sky. Such processions grow more pathetic year by year; it will not be so long now before wondering children will have seen the last. The aging faces of the men, the renewed comradeship, the quick beat of the hearts that remember, the tenderness of those who think upon old sorrows, — all these make the day a lovelier and a sadder festival. So men's hearts were stirred, they knew not why, when they heard the shrill fife and the incessant drum along the quiet Barlow road, and saw the handful of old soldiers marching by. Nobody thought of them as familiar men and neighbors alone, — they were a part of that army which had saved its country. They had taken their lives in their hands and gone out to fight for their country, plain John Stover and Jesse Dean and the rest. No matter if every other day in the year they counted for little or much, whether they were lame-footed and lagging, whether their farms were of poor soil or rich.

The little troop went in slender line along the road; the crowded country wagons and all the people who went afoot followed Martin Tighe's wagon as if it were a great gathering at a country funeral. The route was short, and the long, straggling line marched slowly; it could go no faster than the lame men could walk.

In one of the houses by the roadside an old woman sat by a window, in an old-fashioned black gown, and clean white cap with a prim border which bound her thin, sharp features closely. She had been for a long time looking out eagerly over the snowberry and cinnamon-rose bushes; her face was pressed close to the pane, and presently she caught sight of the great flag as it came down the road.

"Let me see 'em! I 've got to see 'em go by!" she pleaded, trying to rise from her chair alone when she heard the fife, and the women helped her to the door, and held her so that she could stand and wait. She had been an old woman when the war began; she had sent sons and grandsons to the field; they were all gone now. As the men came by, she straightened her bent figure with all the vigor of youth. The fife and drum stopped suddenly; the colors lowered. She did not heed that, but her old eyes flashed and then filled with tears to see the flag going to salute the soldiers' graves. "Thank ye, boys; thank ye!" she cried, in her quavering voice, and they all cheered her. The cheer went back along the straggling line for old Grandmother Dexter, standing there in her front door between the lilacs. It was one of the great moments of the day.

The few old people at the poor-house, too, were waiting to see the show. The keeper's young son, knowing that it was a day of festivity, and not understanding exactly why, had put his toy flag out of the gable window, and there it showed against the gray clapboards like a gay flower. It was the only bit of decoration along the veterans' way, and they stopped and saluted it before they broke ranks and went out to the field corner beyond the poor-farm barn to the bit of ground that held the paupers' unmarked graves. There was a solemn silence while Asa Brown went to the back of Tighe's wagon, where such light freight was carried, and brought two flags, and he and John Stover planted them straight in the green sod. They knew well enough where the right graves were, for these had been made in a corner by themselves, with unwonted sentiment. And so Eben Munson and John Tighe were honored like the rest, both by their flags and by great and unexpected nosegays of spring flowers, daffies and flowering currant and red tulips, which lay on the graves already. John Stover and his comrade glanced at each other curiously while they stood singing, and then laid their own bunches of lilacs down and came away.

Then something happened that almost none of the people in the wagons understood. Martin Tighe's boy, who played the fife, had studied well his part, and on his poor short-winded instrument now sounded taps as well as he could. He had heard it done once in Alton at a soldier's funeral. The plaintive notes called sadly over the fields, and echoed back from the hills. The few veterans could not look at each other; their eyes brimmed up with tears; they could not have spoken. Nothing called back old army days like that. They had a sudden vision of the Virginian camp, the hillside dotted white with tents, the twinkling lights in other camps, and far away the glow of smouldering fires. They heard the bugle call from post to post; they remembered the chilly winter night, the wind in the pines, the laughter of the men. Lights out! Martin Tighe's boy sounded it again sharply. It seemed as if poor Eb Munson and John Tighe must hear it too in their narrow graves.

The procession went on, and stopped here and there at the little graveyards on the farms, leaving their bright flags to flutter through summer and winter rains and snows, and to bleach in the wind and sunshine. When they returned to the church, the minister made an address about the war, and every one listened with new ears. Most of what he said was familiar enough to his listeners; they were used to reading those phrases about the results of the war, the glorious future of the South, in their weekly newspapers; but there never had been such a spirit of patriotism and loyalty waked in Barlow as was waked that day by the poor parade of the remnant of the Barlow soldiers. They sent flags to all the distant graves, and proud were those households who claimed kinship with valor, and could drive or walk away with their flags held up so that others could see that they, too, were of the elect.

III.

It is well that the days are long in the last of May, but John Stover had to hurry more than usual with his evening work, and then, having the longest distance to walk, he was much the latest comer to the Plains store, where his two triumphant friends were waiting for him impatiently on the bench. They also had made excuse of going to the post-office and doing an unnecessary errand for their wives, and were talking together so busily that they had gathered a group about them before the store. When they saw Stover coming, they rose hastily and crossed the road to meet him, as if they were a committee in special session. They leaned against the post-and-board fence, after they had shaken hands with each other solemnly.

"Well, we've had a great day, ain't we, John?" asked Henry Merrill. "You did lead off splendid. We've done a grand thing, now, I tell you. All the folks say we 've got to keep it up every year. Everybody had to have a talk about it as I went home. They say they had no idea we should make such a show. Lord! I wish we 'd begun while there was more of us!"

"That han'some flag was the great feature," said Asa Brown generously. "I want to pay my part for hirin' it. An' then folks was glad to see poor old Martin made o' some consequence."

"There was half a dozen said to me that another year they was goin' to have flags out, and trim up their places somehow or 'nother. Folks has feelin' enough, but you 've got to rouse it," said Merrill.

"I have thought o' joinin' the Grand Army over to Alton time an' again, but it 's a good ways to go, an' then the expense has been o' some consideration," Asa continued. "I don't know but two or three over there. You know, most o' the Alton men nat'rally went out in the rigiments t' other side o' the State line, an' they was in other battles, an' never camped nowheres nigh us. Seems to me we ought to have home feelin' enough to do what we can right here."

"The minister says to me this afternoon that he was goin' to arrange an' have some

talks in the meetin'-house next winter, an'
have some of us tell where we was in the
South; an' one night 't will be about camp
life, an' one about the long marches, an'
then about the battles, — that would take
some time, — an' tell all we could about
the boys that was killed, an' their record,
so they would n't be forgot. He said some
of the folks must have the letters we wrote
home from the front, an' we could make out
quite a history of us. I call Elder Dallas
a very smart man ; he 'd planned it all out
a'ready, for the benefit o' the young folks,
he said," announced Henry Merrill, in a tone
of approval.

"I s'pose there ain't none of us but could
add a little somethin'," answered John Stover
modestly. "'T would re'lly learn the young
folks a good deal. I should be scared numb
to try an' speak from the pulpit. That ain't
what the Elder means, is it? Now I was one
that had a good chance to see somethin' o'
Washin'ton. I shook hands with President
Lincoln, an' I always think I 'm worth
lookin' at for that, if I ain't for nothin' else.
'T was that time I was just out o' hospit'l, an'
able to crawl about some. I 've often told
you how 't was I met him, an' he stopped an'

shook hands an' asked where I 'd been at the front an' how I was gettin' along with my hurts. Well, we 'll see how 't is when winter comes. I never thought I had no gift for public speakin', 'less 't was for drivin' cattle or pollin' the house town-meetin' days. Here! I 've got somethin' in mind. You need n't speak about it if I tell it to ye," he added suddenly. "You know all them han'some flowers that was laid on to Eb Munson's grave an' Tighe's? I mistrusted you thought the same thing I did by the way you looked. They come from Marthy Down's front yard. My woman told me when we got home that she knew 'em in a minute; there wa'n't nobody in town had that kind o' red flowers but her. She must ha' kind o' harked back to the days when she was Marthy Peck. She must have come over with 'em after dark, or else dreadful early in the mornin'."

Henry Merrill cleared his throat. "There ain't nothin' half-way 'bout Mis' Down," he said. "I would n't ha' spoken 'bout this 'less you had led right on to it; but I overtook her when I was gittin' towards home this afternoon, an' I see by her looks she was worked up a good deal; but we talked about how well things had gone off, an' she wanted

to know what expenses we 'd been put to, an'
I told her; and she said she 'd give five dollars any day I 'd stop in for it.   An' then she
spoke right out.   ' I 'm alone in the world,'
says she, ' and I 've got somethin' to do with,
an' I 'd like to have a plain stone put up to
Eb Munson's grave, with the number of his
rigiment on it, an' I 'll pay the bill.   'T ain't
out o' Mr. Down's money,' she says; ' 't is
mine, an' I want you to see to it.'   I said I
would, but we 'd made a plot to git some o'
them soldiers' headstones that 's provided by
the government.   'T was a shame it had been
overlooked so long.   ' No,' says she; ' I 'm
goin' to pay for Eb's myself.'   An' I told
her there would n't be no objection.   Don't
ary one o' you speak about it.   'T would n't
be fair.   She was real well-appearin'.   I
never felt to respect Marthy so before."

" We was kind o' hard on her sometimes,
but folks could n't help it.   I 've seen her
pass Eb right by in the road an' never look
at him when he first come home," said John
Stover.

" If she had n't felt bad, she would n't have
cared one way or t' other," insisted Henry
Merrill.   " 'T ain't for us to judge.   Sometimes folks has to get along in years before

they see things fair. Come; I must be goin'
home.   I 'm tired as an old dog."

"It seemed kind o' natural to be steppin'
out together again. Strange we three got
through with so little damage, an' so many
dropped round us," said Asa Brown. "I 've
never been one mite sorry I went out in old
A Company. I was thinkin' when I was
marchin' to-day, though, that we should all
have to take to the wagons before long an'
do our marchin' on wheels, so many of us
felt kind o' stiff. There 's one thing, — folks
won't never say again that we can't show
no public sperit here in old Barlow."

JIM'S LITTLE WOMAN.

I.

THERE was laughter in the lanes of St. Augustine when Jim returned from a Northern voyage with a Northern wife. He had sailed on the schooner Dawn of Day, one hundred and ninety-two tons burden, with a full cargo of yellow pine and conch-shells. Not that the conch-shells were mentioned in the bill of lading, any more than five handsome tortoise-shells that were securely lashed to the beams in the captain's cabin. These were a private venture of the captain's and Jim's. The Dawn of Day did a great deal of trading with the islands, and it was only when the season of Northern tourists was over that her owners found it more profitable to charter her in the lumber business. It was too hot for bringing any more bananas from Jamaica, the last were half spoiled in the hold; and those Northerners who came excitedly after corals and sprouted cocoanuts and Jamaica baskets, who would gladly pay thirty cents apiece for the best of the conch-shells, brought primarily by way of ballast,— those enthusiastic, money - squandering Northerners had all flown homeward at the first hints of unmistakable summer heat, and market was over for that spring.

St. Augustine is a city of bright sunshine and of cool sea winds, a different place from the steaming-hot, listless-aired Southern ports which Jim knew well, — Kingston and Nassau and the rest. He had sailed between the islands and St. Augustine and Savannah, and made trading voyages round into the Gulf, ever since he ran away to sea on an ancient brigantine bound for Havana, in his early youth. Jim's grandfather was a Northern man by birth, a New-Englander, who had married a Minorcan woman, and settled down in St. Augustine to spend the rest of his days. Their old coquina house near the sea-wall faced one of the narrow lanes that ran up from the water, but it had a wide window in the seaward end, and here Jim remembered that the intemperate old sailor sat and watched the harbor, and criticised the rigging of vessels, and defended his pet orange-tree from the ravages of boys.

His wife died long before he did, and the daughter, Jim's mother, was married, and her husband ran away and never was heard from, and Jim himself was ten years old when he walked at the head of the funeral procession, dimly imagining that the old man had gone up North, and that he was to live again there among the scenes of his youth. There were a few old shipmates walking two by two, who had known the captain in his active life, but they held no definite views about his permanent location in high latitudes. Still, there was a long procession and a handsome funeral; and after a few years Jim's mother died too, a friendly, sad-faced little creature whom everybody lamented. Jim came into port one day after a long absence, expecting to be kissed and cried over and coaxed to church and mended up, to find the old coquina house locked and empty. He shipped again gloomily; there was nothing for him to do ashore; and that year the boys took all the oranges, and people said that the old captain's ghost lived in the house. The bishop stopped Jim one day on the plaza, and told him that he must come to church sometimes for his mother's sake: she was a good little woman, and had said many a prayer for her boy. Did Jim ever say a prayer for himself? It was a hard life, going to sea, and he must not let it be too hard for his soul. "Marry you a good wife soon," said the kind bishop. "Be a good man in your own town; you will be tired of roving and will want a home. God have pity on you, my boy!"

Jim took off his hat reverently, and his frank, bold eyes met the bishop's sad, kind eyes, and fell. He had never really thought what a shocking sort of fellow he was until that moment. He had grown used to his mother's crying, but it was two or three years now since she died. The fellows on board ship were afraid of him when he was surly, and owned him for king when he was pleased to turn life into a joke. He was Northern and Southern by turns, this Southern-born young sailor. He could talk in Yankee fashion like his grandfather until the crew shook the ship's timbers with their laughter. But in all his roving sea-life he had never been to the coast of Maine until this story begins.

The Dawn of Day was a slow sailer, and what wind she had was only a light south-westerly breeze. Every other day was a dead calm, and so they drifted up the Northern coast as if the Gulf Stream alone impelled them, making for the island of Mount Desert with their yellow pine for house-finishing; and somewhere near Boothbay Harbor their provisions got low, and the drinking-water was too bad altogether, and there was nothing else left to drink, so the captain put in for supplies. They could not get up to the inner harbor next the town, but came to anchor near a little village when the wind fell at sundown. There were some houses in sight, dotted along the shore, and a long, low building at the water's edge, close to the little bay. Jim and the captain and another man pulled ashore to see what could be done about the water-casks, and the old water-tank, which had been rusty, was leaky and good for nothing when they first put to sea.

Jim went ashore, and presently put his head into a window of the long, low building; there were a dozen young people there, and two or three men, with heaps of lobster shells and long rows of shining cans. It was a lobster-canning establishment, and work was going on after hours. Somebody screamed when Jim's shaggy head and broad shoulders shut out the little daylight that was left, and a bevy of girls laughed provokingly; but one of them — Jim thought she was a child until she came quite close to him — asked what he wanted, and listened with intelligent patience until he had quite explained his errand. It proved easy to get somebody to solder up the water-tank, and in spite of the other girls this little red-haired, white-faced creature caught her hat from a nail by the door, and went off with Jim to find the solderer, who lived a quarter of a mile down the shore.

Jim thought of the old bishop many times as he walked decently along by the little woman's side. He thought of his mother, too, and how she used to cry over him; he never pitied her for it before. He remembered his cross old grandfather and those stories about the North, and by a strange turn of memory he mentally cursed the boys who came to steal the old man's oranges, there in the garden of his own empty little coquina house. What a thing to have a good little warm-hearted wife of his own! Jim felt as if he had been set on fire; as if something hindered him from ever feeling like himself again; as if he must forever belong to this little bit of a woman, who almost ran, trying to keep up with his great rolling sea strides along the road. She had a clear, pleasant little voice, and kept looking up at him, asking now and then something about the voyage as if she were used to voyages, and seemed pleased with his gruff, shy answers. He heaved a great sigh when they came to the solderer's door.

The solderer came out and walked back with them, saying that his tools were all at the factory. He told Jim that there was the best cold spring on the coast convenient to the schooner, just beyond the factory, and a good grocery store near by. There was no reason for going up to Boothbay Harbor and losing all that time in the morning, and Jim's heart grew light at the news. He sent the solderer off to the schooner, and stayed ashore himself. The captain had already heard about the grocery, and had gone there. The grumbling member of the crew, who was left in the boat, looked back with heart-felt astonishment to see Jim sit down on a piece of ship timber beside that strange little woman, and begin to talk with her as if they were old friends. It was a clear June evening, the sky was pale yellow in the west, and on the high land above the shore a small jangling bell rang in its white steeple. A salt breath of sea wind ruffled the smooth water. The lights went out in the canning factory and twinkled with bright reflections from the schooner. The solderer finished his work on board, and was put ashore close to his own house; as for the captain, he remained with some new-made friends at the grocery.

They wondered on the deck of the Dawn of Day what had come over Jim; they laughed and joked, and thought that he might have found one of his relations about whom he had told the Yankee stories. As long as there was any light to see, there he sat, an erect, great fellow, with the timid-looking little woman like a child by his side. The captain came off late, and in a state unbefitting the laws of Maine, and Jim came with him, sober, pleasant, but holding his head in that high, proud way which forbade any craven soul from putting an unwelcome question.

The next morning, when the wind rose, the Dawn of Day put out to sea again. Somebody besides Jim may have noticed that a white handkerchief fluttered at one of the canning-factory windows, but nobody knew that it meant so much to Jim as this: the little woman was going to marry him, and promised by that signal to come to Mount Desert to meet him. They had no more time for courtship; it was now or never with the quick-tempered fellow. Little Martha did not dare to promise until she had thought it over that night; but she was a lonely orphan, and had no ties to keep her there. Jim had told her about his home and his orange-tree in the South, and when morning came she had thought it over and said yes, and then even cried a little to see the old schooner go out to sea. She said yes because she loved him; because she had never thought that anybody would fall in love with her, she was so small and queer, and not like the rest of the girls. Jim had certainly waved his handkerchief in reply; and as Marty remembered that, she felt in her pocket for a queer smooth shell to make herself sure that she was not dreaming. Jim had carried this shell in his pocket for good luck, as his strange old seafaring grandfather had done before him, and by it he plighted his faith and troth. Before they sighted Monhegan, running far out to catch the

wind, he told the skipper that he was going
to be married, and expected to carry his wife
down to St. Augustine in the Dawn of Day.
The skipper swore roundly, but Jim was
the ablest man aboard, and had been shipped
that voyage as first mate. They were short-
handed, and he was in Jim's power in many
ways. There was a wedding, before the
week was out, at a minister's house, and Jim
gave the minister's wife a pretty basket of
shells besides what Marty considered to be a
generous wedding fee. He had bought a
suit of ready-made clothes before he went to
the cousin's house where the little woman
had promised to wait for him. Marty did
not explain to this cousin that she had only
seen her lover once in the twilight. She
wondered if people would think Jim rough
and strange, that was all ; but Jim for once
was in possession of small savings, and when
he came, so tall and dark, shaven and
shorn and dressed like other people, she fell
to crying with joy and excitement, and had
much difficulty in explaining to her lover
that it was nothing but happiness and love
that had brought such tears. And after the
yellow pine was on the wharf, and the conch-
shells sold at unexpected rates to a dealer in

curiosities at Bar Harbor, who got news of them, and after much dickering gave but a meagre price for the tortoises also, the Dawn of Day set forth again southward with dried fish and flour from Portland, where, with his share of the conch-shell gains, Jim had given his wife such a pleasuring as he thought a lord who had an earldom at his back might give his fair lady.

When the crew first caught sight of Jim's small, red-headed, and pale-faced wife, the discrepancy in the size of the happy couple was more than could be silently borne. Jim always spoke of her as his little woman, and Jim's little woman she was to the world in general. She was as proud-spirited as he. She seldom scolded, but she could grow pale in the face and keep silence if things went wrong. The schooner was a different place on that return voyage. They had the captain's cabin, and she made it look pretty with her girlish arts. She mended everybody's clothes, and took care of the schooner's boy when he was sick with a fever turn,— a hard-faced little chap, who had run about from ship to ship, just as Jim had; and though the wind failed them most of the time going south, they were all sorry when they reached St. Augustine bar. The last Sunday night of all, Jim's little woman got out her Moody and Sankey song-book for the last time, and sang every tune she knew in her sweet, old-fashioned voice. She was rough in her way sometimes, but the crew of the Dawn of Day kept to the level of its best manners in her hearing all the time she was on board. As they lay out beyond the bar, waiting for enough water to get in, she strained her eyes to see her future home. There was the queer striped light-house, with its corkscrew pattern of black and white, and far beyond were the tall, slender towers of a town that looked beautiful against the sunset, and a long, low shore, white with sand and green here and there with a new greenness which she believed to be orange-trees. She may have had a pang of homesickness for the high ledgy pasture shores at home, but nobody ever guessed it. If ever anybody in this world married for love, it was Jim's little woman.

II.

It was not long before the dismal little, boarded-up, spidery coquina house was as clean as a whistle, with new glass windows, and fresh whitewash inside and yellow wash outside ; with curtains and rugs and calico cushions, and a shining cooking-stove, on which such meals were concocted as Jim never dreamed of having for his own. The little woman had a small inheritance of housekeeping goods, which had been packed into the schooner's hold ; luckily these had been in charge of the Northeast Harbor, cousin ; as Jim said, they had to get married, for everything came right and there was nothing else to do. He seemed as happy as the day was long, and for once was glad to be ashore. They went together to do their marketing, and he showed her the gray old fort one afternoon and the great hotels with the towers. In narrow St. George Street, under the high flower-lined balconies, everybody seemed to know Jim, and they had to spend much time in doing a trifling errand. Go into St. George Street when she would, the narrow thoroughfare was filled with people, and dark-eyed men and women leaned from the balconies and talked to passers-by in a strange lingo which Jim seemed to know. People laughed a good deal as they passed, and the little woman feared that they might think that she was queer-looking. She hated to be so little when Jim himself was so big; but somehow the laughter all stopped after one day, when a man with an evil face said something in a mocking voice, and Jim, blazing with wrath, caught him by the waist and threw him over the fence into a garden.

"They laugh to think o' me getting so small a wife," said Jim frankly one day, in one of his best moods. "One o' the boys thought I 'd raised me a fambly while we was gone, and said I 'd done well for a little gal, but where was the old lady. I promised I 'd bring him round to supper some night, too; he 's a good fellow," added Jim. "We 'll have some o' your clam fritters, and near about stuff him to death."

The summer days flew by, and to everybody's surprise Jim lived the life of a sober man. He went to work on one of the new harbor jetties at his wife's recommendation, and did good service. He gave Marty his pay, and was amused and astonished to see how far she made it go. With plenty of good food, he seemed to have lost his craving for drink in great measure ; and they had two boarders, steady men and Jim's mates, for there was plenty of room ; and the little woman was endlessly busy and happy. Jim had his dark Spanish days with a black scowl, and Marty had her own hot tempers, that came, as she said, of the color of her hair. Like other people, they had their great and small trials and troubles, but these always ended in Marty's stealing into her husband's lap as he sat by the window in his grandfather's old chair. The months went by, and winter came, and spring and their baby came, and then they were happier than ever. Jim, for his mother's sake, carried him to the old bishop to be christened, and all the neighbors flocked in afterward and were feasted. But there was no mistake about it, Jim drank more than was good for him that day in his pride and joy, and had an out and out spree while the baby's mother was helpless in bed ; it was the first great worry and sorrow of their married life. The neighbors came and sat with Marty and told her all about him ; and she got well as fast as she could, and went out, pale and weak, after him, and found Jim in a horrid den and brought him home. But he was sorry, and said it was all the other fellows' fault, and a fellow must have his fling. The little woman sighed, and cried too when there was nobody to see her. She had never believed, though she had had warnings enough, that there was any need of being anxious about Jim. Men were different from women. Yet anybody so strong and masterful ought surely to master himself. But things grew worse and worse; and at last, when the old schooner, with a rougher-looking crew than usual, came into the harbor, the baby's father drank with them all oné night, and shipped with them next morning, and sailed away, in spite of tears and coaxing, on a four months' voyage. Marty had only three cents in her thrifty little purse at the time. It was a purse that her mate at the canning factory gave her the Christmas before she was married. All the simple, fearless old life came up before her as she looked at it. The giver had cried when they parted, and had written once or twice, but the last letter had been long unanswered. Marty had lost all her heart now about writing; she must wait until Jim was at home and steady again.

Alas, the months went by, and it seemed as if that time would never come.

Jim came home at last, drunk and scolding, and when he went away again with the schooner it would have been a relief to be rid of him, if it were not for the worry. He did not look so strong and well as he used. Under the tropic skies his habits were murdering him slowly. The only comfort Marty could take in him was when he lay asleep, with the black hair curling about his smooth white forehead, and that pleasant boyish look coming out on his face instead of the Spanish scowl. The little woman lost her patience at last, and began to wear a scowl too. She was a peppery little body, and sometimes Jim felt himself aggrieved and called her sharp names in foreign tongues. He had a way of bringing his cronies home to supper when she was tired, and ordering her about contemptuously before the low-faced men. At last, one night, they made such a racket that a group of idle negroes clustered about the house, laughing and jeering at the company within. Marty's Northern fury rose like a winter gale; she was vexed by the taunts of a woman who lived up the lane, who used to come out and sit on her high blue balcony and spy all their goings on, and call the baby *poor child* so that his mother could hear. Jim's little woman drove the ribald company out of doors that night, and they quailed, drunk as they were, before her angry eyes. They chased the negroes in their turn, and went off shouting and swearing down the bayside. They tried to walk on the sea-wall, and one man fell over and was too drunk to find his way ashore, and lay down on the wet, shelly mud. The tide came up and covered Joe Black, and that was the last of him, which was not without its comfort, for Jim stayed humbly at home, and tried to make his wife think better of him, for days together. He had won an out and out bad name in the last year. Nobody would give him a good job ashore now, so that he had to go to sea. He was apt to lead his companions astray, and go off on a frolic with too many followers. Yet everybody liked Jim, and greeted him warmly when he came ashore ; and he could walk as proudly as ever through the town when he had had just drink enough to make him think well of himself and everybody else. He dodged round many a corner to avoid meeting the bishop, that good, gray-haired man with the kind, straightforward eyes.

Marty made a good bit of money in the season. She liked to work, and was always ready to do anything there was to do, — scrubbing or washing and ironing or sewing, — and she came to be known in the town for her quickness and power of work. While Jim was away she always got on well and saved something; but when he came in from his voyages things went from bad to worse; and after a while there was news of another baby, and the first one was cross and masterful; and the woman up the lane, in her rickety blue balcony, did nothing but spy discomforts with her mocking eyes.

Jim was more like himself that last week before he went to sea than for a long time before. He seemed sorry to go, and kept astonishingly sober all the last few days, and picked the oranges and planted their little vegetable garden without being asked, and made Marty a new bench for her tubs that she had only complained of needing once or twice. He worked at loading the schooner down at the sawmill, and came home early in the evening, and Marty began to believe she had at last teased him and shamed him into being decent. She even thought of writing to her friend in Boothbay after two years' silence, she had such new hopes about being happy and prosperous again. She talked to Jim about that night when they first saw each other, and Jim was not displeased when she got the lucky shell out of a safe hiding-place and showed him that she had kept it. They looked each other in the face as they seldom did now, and each knew that the other thought the shell had brought little luck of late. Jim sat down by the window and pulled Marty into his lap, and she began to cry the minute her head was on his shoulder. Life had been so hard. What had come over Jim?

"That old bishop o' my mother's," faltered Jim. "He's been givin' it to me; he catched me out by the old gates, and he says, 'Jim, you're goin' to break your little woman's heart.' Was that so, Marty?"

Marty said nothing; she only nodded her head against his shoulder and cried like a child. She could feel his warm shoulder through his coat, and in a minute he asked her again, "Was that so, Marty?" And Marty, for answer, only cried a little less. It was night, and Jim was going away in the morning. The crickets were chirping in the garden. Somebody went along the sea-wall singing, and Jim and his little woman sat there by the window.

" The devil gets me," said Jim at last, in a sober-minded Northern way that he had sometimes. " There 's an awful wild streak in me. I ain't goin' to have you cry like mother always done. I 'm goin' to settle down an' git a steady job ashore, after this one v'y'ge to the islands. I 'm goin' to fetch ye home the handsomest basketful of shells that ever you see, an' then I 'm done with shipping, I am so."

" 'T ain't me only; 't is them poor little babies," said Marty, in a tired, hopeful little voice. She had done crying now. She felt somehow as if the reward for all her patience and misery was coming.

" I would n't go off an' leave ye now, as things be with ye," said Jim, " but you see we need the money; an' then I 've shipped, and the old man 's got my word. I 'm stout to work aboard ship, an' he knows it, the cap'n does. The old bishop he warned me against the cap'n; he said if 't wa'n't for him I 'd be master o' a better vessel myself. He works me hard an' keeps me under. I do believe the bishop 's right about him, and I 'd kept clear from drink often if 't wa'n't for the old man."

" *You 've* kep' you under," said honest Marty. "Nobody ain't master over you when it comes to that. *You 've* got to set your mind right against drink an' the cap'n, Jim."

"It 's so cursed hot in them islands," Jim explained. "You get spent, and have to work right through everything; but I give you my honest word I 'll bring you home my pay this trip."

At which promise the little woman gave a pleased sigh, and moved her head as if for sheer comfort. She tried to think whether there was anything else she could have done to the poor clothes in his battered sea-chest; then she fell asleep. When she waked in the morning, Jim had laid her on the bed like a child, and spread an old shawl over her, and had gone. At high tide in the early morning the schooner Dawn of Day had come up from the sawmill wharf with a tug, and sent a boat ashore for Jim. Marty had never missed him as she did that morning; she had never felt so sure of his loving her, and had waked thinking to find herself still in his arms as she had fallen asleep. There stood the empty chair by the window; and through the window, over beyond the marshes, she could see the gray sails of the schooner standing out to sea. Oh, Jim! Jim! and their little child was crying in the crib, like a hungry bird in its nest — the poor little fellow! — and calling his father with pleading confidence. Jim liked the brave little lad. When he was sober, he always dressed up on Sundays and took little Jim and his mother for a walk. Sometimes they went to the old Spanish burying-ground, and Jim used to put the baby on his grandfather's great tombstone, built strong over his grave like a little house, and pick the moss from the epitaph with his great sea jack-knife. His mother had paid for the tomb. She was laid at one side of it, but Jim had never built any tomb for her. He meant to do it, some time, and Marty always picked some flowers and green sprigs and laid them on the grave with its bits of crumbling coquina at the head and foot.

In spite of a pain at her heart, and a foreboding that Jim would never come back from his unwilling voyage, the little woman went up the lane boldly that late morning after he sailed; she no longer feared the mocking smile and salutation of the neighbor in the balcony. She went to her work cheerfully, and sang over it one of her Moody and Sankey hymns. She made a pleasure for the other women who were washing too, with her song and her cheerful face. She was such a little woman that she had a box to stand on while she washed, but there never was such a brisk little creature for work.

III.

Somehow everything prospered in the next two months until the new baby came. Some young women hired all her spare rooms, and paid well for their lodging, besides being compassionate and ready to give a little lift with the housework when they had the time. Marty had never laid by so much money before, and often spoke with pride of her handsome husband to the lodgers, who had never seen him: they were girls from the North, and one of them had once worked in a canning factory. One day Marty wrote to her own old friend, and asked her to come down by the steamer to Savannah, and then the rest of the way by rail, to make her a long visit. There was plenty of hotel work in the town; her lodgers themselves got good wages on George Street.

Jim was not skilled with his pen; he never wrote to her when he went away, but ever since they were married Marty always had a dream one of the nights while he was gone, in which she saw the schooner's white sails against a blue sky, and Jim himself walking the deck to and fro, holding his head high, as he did when he was pleased. She always saw the Dawn of Day coming safe into harbor in this dream; but one day she thought with a sudden chill that for this voyage the good omen was lacking. Jim had taken the lucky shell along; at any rate, she could not find it after he went away; that was a little thing, to be sure, but it gave some comfort until one morning, in shaking and brushing the old chair by the seaward window, out dropped the smooth white shell. The luck had stayed with her instead of going with poor Jim, and the time was drawing near for his return. The new baby was a dear little girl; she knew that Jim wanted a girl baby, and now, with the girl baby in her arms, she began her weary watch for white sails beyond the marshes.

The winter days dawned with blue skies and white clouds sailing over; the town began to fill with strangers. As she got

strong enough there was plenty of work waiting for her. The two babies were a great
deal too large and heavy for their little
mother to tend; they seemed to take after
Jim in size, and to grow apace, and Marty
took the proud step of hiring help. There
was a quiet little colored girl, an efficient
midget of a creature, who had minded babies
for a white woman in Baya Lane, and was not
without sage experience. Marty had bought
a perambulator the year before from a woman
at one of the boarding-houses, who did not
care to carry it North. When she left the
hired help in charge that first morning, and
hurried away to her own work, the neighbor
of the blue balcony stood in her lower doorway and bade her a polite good-morning.
But Jim's little woman's eyes glittered with
strange light as she hurried on in the shadow
of the high wall, where the orange boughs
hung over, and beyond these, great branches
laden with golden clusters of ripening lo-
quats. She had not looked out of the seaward window, as she always liked to do
before she left the house, and she was sorry,
but there was no time to go back.

The old city of St. Augustine had never
been more picturesque and full of color than

it was that morning. Its narrow thorough-
fares, with the wide, overhanging upper balconies that shaded them, were busy and gay.
Strangers strolled along, stopping in groups
before the open fronts of the fruit shops,
or were detained by eager venders of flowers
and orange - wood walking - sticks. There
were shining shop windows full of photo-
graphs and trinkets of pink shell-work and
palmetto. There were pink feather fans,
and birds in cages, and strange shapes and
colors of flowers and fruits, and stuffed
alligators. The narrow street was full of
laughter and the sound of voices. Lumber-
ing carriages clattered along the palmetto
pavement, and boys and men rode by on
quick, wild little horses as if for dear life,
and to the frequent peril of persons on foot.
Sometimes these small dun or cream-colored
marsh tackeys needed only a cropped mane
to prove their suspected descent from the
little steeds of the Northmen, or their cousin-
ship to those of the Greek friezes ; they were,
indeed, a part of the picturesqueness of the
city.

The high gray towers of the beautiful
Ponce de Leon Hotel, with their pointed red
roofs, were crowned with ornaments like the

berries of the chinaberry-trees, and Marty looked up at them as she walked along, and at the trees themselves, hung with delicate green leaves like a veil. Spring seemed to come into the middle of summer in that country; it was the middle of February, but the season was very early. There was a mocking-bird trying its voice here and there in the gardens. The wind-tattered bananas, like wrecked windmills, were putting out fresh green leaves among their ragged ones. There were roses and oranges in bloom, and the country carts were bringing in new vegetables from beyond the old city gates; green lettuces and baskets of pease and strawberries, and trails of golden jasmine were everywhere about the gray town. Down at the foot of the narrow lanes the bay looked smooth and blue, and white sails flitted by as you stood and looked. The great bell of the old cathedral had struck twelve, and as Marty entered the plaza, busy little soul that she was and in a hurry as usual, she stopped, full of a never outgrown Northern wonder at the foreign sights and sounds, — the tall palmettoes; the riders with their clinking spurs; the gay strangers; the three Sisters of St. Joseph, in their quaint garb of black and white, who came soberly from their parish school close by. Jim's little woman looked more childlike than ever. She always wore a short dress about her work, and her short crop of red curly hair stood out about her pale face under the round palmetto hat. She had been thinking of Jim, and of her afternoon's affairs, and of a strange little old negro woman who had been looking out of a doorway on George Street, as she passed. It seemed to Marty as if this old withered creature could see ghosts in the street instead of the live passers-by. She never looked at anybody who passed, but sometimes she stood there for an hour looking down the street and mumbling strange words to herself. Jim's little woman was not without her own superstitions; she had been very miserable of late about Jim, and especially since she found his lucky shell. If she could only see him coming home in her dream; she had always dreamed of him before!

Suddenly she became aware that all the little black boys were running through the streets like ants, with single bananas, or limp, over-ripe bunches of a dozen; and she turned quickly, running a few steps in her eagerness to see the bay. Why had she not looked that way before? There at the pier were the tall masts and the black and green hull of the Dawn of Day. She had come in that morning. Marty felt dizzy, and had to lean for a minute against the old cathedral doorway. There was a drone of music inside; she heard it and lost it; then it came again as her faintness passed, and she ran like a child down the street. Her hat blew off and she caught it with one hand, but did not stop to put it on again. The long pier was black with people down at the end next the schooner, and they were swarming up over the side and from the deck. There were red and white parasols from the hotel in the middle of the crowd, and a general hurry and excitement. Everybody but Marty seemed to have known hours before that the schooner was in. Perhaps she ought to go home first; Jim might be there. Now she could see the pretty Jamaica baskets heaped on the top of the cabin, and the shining colors of shells, and green plumes of sprouted cocoanuts for planting, and the great white branches and heads of coral; she could smell the ripe fruit in the hold, and catch sight of some of the crew. At last she was on the gangway, and somebody on deck swore a great oath under his breath. "Boys," he said, in a loud whisper, "here's Jim's little woman!" and two or three of them dropped quickly between decks and down into the hold rather than face her. When she came on board, there was nobody to be seen but the hard-faced cabin-boy whom she had taken care of in a fever as they came down from Boothbay. He had been driving a brisk trade with some ladies down in the captain's cabin.

"Where's Jim gone?" said Marty, looking at him fiercely with her suspicious gray eyes.

"You'd better go ask the cap'n," said the boy. He was two years older than when she first knew him, but he looked much the same, only a little harder. Then he remembered how good Marty had been to him, and that the "old man" was in a horrid temper. He took hold of Marty's thin, freckled, hard-worked little hand, and got her away aft into the shadow and behind the schooner's large boat. "Look here," he faltered, "I'm awful sorry, Marty; it's too bad, but — Jim's dead."

Jim's wife looked the young fellow straight

in the face, as if she were thinking about something else, and had not heard him.

"Here, sit right down on this box," said the boy. But Marty would not sit down; she had a dull sense that she must not stay any longer, and that the sun was hot, and that she could not walk home along the sea-wall alone.

"I 'll go home with you," said the boy, giving her a little push; but she took hold of his hand and did not move.

"Say it over again what you said," she insisted, looking more and more strange; her short red hair was blowing in the wind all about her face, and her eyes had faded and faded until they looked almost white.

"Jim 's dead," said the hard-looking boy, who thought he should cry himself, and wished that he were out of such a piece of business. The people who had come to chaffer for shells began to look at them and to whisper. "He 's dead. He — well, he was as steady as a gig 'most all the time we was laying off o' Kingston, and the ol' man could n't master him to go an' drink by night; and Jim he would n't let me go ashore; told me he 'd 'bout kill me; an' I sassed him up an' down for bossin', and he never hit me a clip back nor

nothin': he was queer this voyage. I
never see him drunk but once, — when we
first put into Nassau, — and then he was
a-cryin' afterwards; and into Kingston he
got dizzy turns, and was took sick and laid
in his bunk while we was unloadin'. 'T was
blazin' hot. *You* never see it so hot; an'
the ol' man told how 't was his drinkin' the
water that give him a fever; an' when he
went off his head, the old man got the hospit'l folks, an' they lugged him ashore
a-ravin'; an' he was just breathin' his last
the day we sailed. We see his funeral as
we come out o' harbor; they was goin' out
buryin' of him right off. I ain't seen it
myself, but Jim Peet was the last ashore,
an' he asked if 't was our Jim, an' they said
't was. They 'd sent word in the mornin'
he was 'bout gone, and we might 's well
sail 'f we was ready."

"Jim Peet saw his funeril?" gasped the
little woman. "He felt sure 't was *Jim?*"

"Yes 'm. You come home 'long o' me;
folks is lookin'," said the boy. "Come,
now; I 'll tell you some more goin' along."

Marty came with him through the crowd.
She held her hat in her hand, and she went
feeling her way, as if she were blind, down

the gangway plank. When they reached
the shore and had gone a short distance,
she turned, and told the lad that he need
not come any farther; if he would bring
his clothes over before the schooner sailed,
she would mend them all up nice for him.
Then she crept slowly along Bay Street
bareheaded; the sun on the water at the
right blinded her a little. Sometimes she'
stopped and leaned against the fence or a
house front, and so at last got home. It
was midday, there was not a soul in the
house, and Jim was dead.

*That night she dreamed of a blue sky,
and white sails, and Jim, with his head up,
walking the deck, as he came into harbor.*

IV.

All the townsfolk who lived by the water-
side and up and down the lanes, and many
of the strangers at the hotels, heard of poor
Marty's trouble. Her poorest neighbors
were the first to send a little purse that they
had spared out of their small savings and
earnings; then by and by some of the hotel

people and those who were well to do in the
town made her presents of money and of
clothes for the children; and even the spy-
ing neighbor of the balcony brought a cake,
and some figs, all she had on her tree, the
night the news was known, and put them
on the table, and was going away without a
word, but Marty ran after her and kissed
her, for the poor soul's husband had been
lost at sea, and so they could weep together.
But after the dream everybody said that
Marty was hurt in her mind by the shock.
She could not cry for her own loss when
she was told over and over about her neighbor's man; she only said to the people who
came that they were very kind, and she was
seeing trouble, but she was sure that Jim
would come back; she knew it by her
dream. They must wait and see. She
could not force them to take their money
back, and when she grew too tired and un-
strung to plead about it any longer, she put.
it together in a little box, and hid it on a
high cupboard shelf in the chimney. There
was a wonderful light of hope in her face in
these days; she kept the little black girl to
tend the two babies, and kept on with her
own work. Everybody said that she was

not quite right in the brain. She was often pointed out to strangers in that spring season, a quaint figure, so small, so wan, and battling against the world for her secret certainty and hope.

Never a man's footstep came by the house at night that she did not rouse and start with her heart beating wildly; but one, two, three months went by, and still she was alone. Once she went across the bay to the lighthouse island, — babies, baby-carriage, the small hired help, and all, — and took the railway that leads down to the south beach. It was a holiday, and she hoped that from this southern point she might look far seaward, and catch sight of the returning sails of the old schooner. She would not listen to her own warnings that Jim had plenty of ways of getting home besides waiting for the Dawn of Day. Those who saw the little company strike out across the sand to the beach laughed at the sight. The hired help pushed the empty perambulator with all the strength she could muster through the deep white sand, and over the huge green, serpent-like vines that wound among the low dunes. Marty carried the baby and tugged the little boy by the other hand, and sat down at the edge of the beach all alone, while the children played in the sand or were pushed to and fro. She strained her eyes after sails, but only a bark was in sight to the northward beyond the bar, and a brigantine was beating southward, and far beyond that was a schooner going steadily north, and it was not the Dawn of Day. All the time Jim's little woman kept saying to herself: "I had the dream; I had the dream. Jim will come home." But as this miserable holiday ended, and they left the great sand desert and the roar of the sea behind them, she felt a new dread make her heart heavier than ever it had been before; perhaps even the dream was mocking her, and he was dead indeed.

Then Marty had need of comfort. She believed that as long as she kept faith in her omen it would come true, and yet her faith slowly ebbed in spite of everything. It was a cruel test, and she could not work as she used; she felt the summer heat as she never had before. All her old associations with the cool Northern sea-coast began to call her to come home. She wondered if it would not do to go North for a while and wait for Jim there. The old friend had written that next winter she would come down for a visit, and somehow Marty longed to get home for a while, and then they could come South together; but at last she felt too tired and weak, and gave up the thought. If it were not for the children, she could go to Jamaica and find out all about Jim. She had sent him more than one letter to Kingston, but no answer came. Perhaps she would wait now until next summer, and then go North with Lizzie.

In midsummer the streets are often empty at midday, and the old city seems deserted. Marty sometimes took the children and sat with them in the plaza, where it was shady. Often in the spring they all wandered up the white pavement of the street by the great hotel to see the gay Spanish flags, and to hear the band play in the gardens of the Ponce de Leon; but the band did not play as it used. Marty used to tell the eldest of the children that when his father came home he would take him sailing in the bay, and the little fellow got a touching fashion of asking every morning if his father were coming that day. It was a sad summer, — a sad summer. Marty knew that her neighbors thought her a little crazed; at last she

wondered if they were not right. She began
to be homesick, and at last she had to give
up work altogether. She hated the glare of
the sun and the gay laughter of the black
people; when she heard the sunset gun
from the barracks it startled her terribly.
She almost doubted sometimes whether she
had really dreamed the dream.

One afternoon when the cars stopped at
the St. Augustine station, Marty was sitting
in the old chair by the seaward window,
looking out and thinking of her sorrow.
There was a vine about the window that
flickered a pretty shadow over the floor
in the morning, and it was dancing and
waving in the light breeze that blows like a
long, soft breath, and then stops at sundown.
She saw nothing in the bay but a few small
pleasure-boats, and there was nothing beyond
the bar. News had come some time before
that the Dawn of Day had gone North
again with yellow pine, and the few other
schooners that came now and then to the
port were away on the sea, nobody knew
where. They came in as if they dropped
out of the sky, as far as Marty was con-
cerned. She thought about Jim as she sat
there; how good he was before he sailed

that last time, and had really tried to keep his promise on board ship, according to the cabin-boy's story. Somehow Jim was like the moon to her at first; his Spanish blood and the Church gave an unknown side to his character that was always turned away; but another side shone fair through his Northern traits, and of late she had understood him as she never had before. She used to be too smart-spoken and too quick with him; she saw it all now; a quick man ought to have a wife with head enough to keep her own temper for his sake. "I couldn't help being born red-headed," thought Marty with a wistful smile, and then she was dreaming and dozing, and fell fast asleep.

The train had stopped in the station, and among the strangers who got out was a very dark young man, with broad shoulders, and of uncommon height. He was smartly dressed in a sort of uniform, and looked about him with a familiar smile as he strolled among the idlers on the platform. Suddenly somebody caught him by the hand, with a shout, and there was an eager crowd about him in a minute. "Jim! Here's dead Jim!" cried some one, with a shrill laugh, and there was a great excitement.

· "No," said Jim, "I ain't dead. What's the matter with you all? I 've been up North with the best yacht you ever see; first we went cruisin' in the Gulf an' over to Martinique. Why, my wife know'd I was goin'. I had a fellow write her from Kingston, an' not to expect me till I come. I give him a quarter to do it."

" *She* thinks you 're dead. No; other folks says so, an' she won't. Word come by the schooner that you was dead in hospit'l, of a Jamaica fever," somebody explained in the racket and chatter.

"They always was a pack o' fools on that leaky old Dawn o' Day," said Jim contemptuously, looking down the steep, well-clothed precipice of himself to the platform. "I don't sail with those kind o' horse-marines any more."

Then he thought of Marty with sudden intensity. "She never had got his letter!" He shouldered his great valise and strode away; there was something queer about his behavior; nobody could keep up with his long steps and his quick runs, and away he went toward home.

Jim's steps grew softer and slower as he went down the narrow lane; he saw the little house, and its door wide open. The woman in the blue balcony saw him, and gave a little scream, as if he were a ghost. The minute his foot touched the deep-worn coquina step, Marty in her sleep heard it and opened her eyes. She had dreamed again at last of the blue sky and white sails; she opened her eyes to see him standing there, with his head up, in the door. Jim not dead! not dead! but Jim looking sober, and dressed like a gentleman, come home at last!

That evening they walked up Bay Street to King Street, and round the plaza, and home again through George Street, making a royal progress, and being stopped by everybody. They told the story over and over of its having been another sailor from a schooner, poor fellow! who had died in Kingston that day, alone in hospital. Jim himself had gone down to the gates of death and turned back. There was a yacht in harbor that had lost a hand, and the owner saw handsome Jim on the pier, looking pale and unfriended, and took a liking to him, and found how well he knew the Gulf and the islands, so they struck a bargain at once. They had cruised far south and then north again, and Jim only had leave to come home for a few days to bring away his little woman and the children, because he was to keep with the yacht, and spend the summer cruising in Northern waters. Marty had always been wishing to make a visit up in Maine, where she came from. Jim fingered his bright buttons and held his head higher than ever, as if he had been told that she felt proud to show him to her friends. He looked down at little Marty affectionately; it was very queer about that dream and other people's saying he was dead. He must buy her a famous new rig before they started to go North; she looked worn out and shabby. It seemed all a miracle to Marty; but her dream was her dream, and she felt as tall as Jim himself as she remembered it. As they went home at sunset, they met the bishop, who stopped before them and looked down at the little woman, and then up at Jim.

"So you're doing well now, my boy?" he said good humoredly, to the great, smiling fellow. "Ah, Jim, many's the prayer your pious mother said for you, and I myself not a few. Come to Mass and be a Christian man for the sake of her. God bless you, my children!" and the good man went his wise and kindly way, not knowing all their story either, but knowing well and compassionately the sorrows and temptations of poor humanity.

It seemed to Marty as if she had had time to grow old since the night Jim went away and left her sleeping, but the long misery was quickly fading out of her mind, now that he was safe at home again. In a few days more, the old coquina house was carefully shut and locked for the summer, and they gave the key to the woman of the blue balcony. The morning that they started northward, Marty caught a glimpse of the Dawn of Day coming in through the mist over the harbor bar. She wisely said nothing to Jim; she thought with apprehension of the captain's usual revelry the night he came into port. She took a last look at the tall light-house, and remembered how it had companioned her with its clear ray through many a dark and anxious night. Then she thought joyfully how soon she should see the far-away spark on Monhegan, and the bright light of Seguin, and presently the towers of St. Augustine were left out of sight behind the level country and the Southern pines.

THE FAILURE OF DAVID BERRY.

Mr. David Berry kept his shop in a small wooden building in his own yard, and worked steadily there a great many years, being employed by a large manufacturing company in Lynn at soling and heeling men's boots. There were many such small shoe shops as his scattered among the villages and along the country roads. Most of the farmers knew something of the shoe-making trade, and they and their sons worked in their warm little shops in winter when they had nothing else to do, and so added a good deal of ready money to their narrow incomes. The great Lynn teams, piled high with clean wooden shoe boxes, came and went along the highways at regular times, to deliver and collect the work. Many of the women bound shoes, and sometimes in pleasant weather half a dozen friends came together with their bundles, and had a bit of friendly gossip while they stitched. The little shops were only large enough for the shoe benches, with shiny leather seats and trays of small tools, sprinkled with steel and wooden shoe pegs and snarled with waxed ends; for their whetstones and lapstones and lasts, and the rusty, raging little stoves, with a broken chair or two, where idlers or customers could make themselves permanently comfortable. No woman's broom or duster had any right to invade the pungent, leathery, dusty, pasty abodes of shoemaking; these belonged wholly to men, and had a rudeness akin to savagery, together with a delightful, definite sort of hospitality as warm as the atmosphere itself. If there were not a life-sustaining broken pane of glass somewhere, the door had to be left ajar. There were apt to be apples on the high window ledges, and any one might choose the best and eat it, and throw the core down among the chips of leather. The shoemaker usually had a dog, which wagged an impartial tail at each new-comer; for the shoemaker always sat in the same place, and society came and found him there, and told news and heard it, and went away again. There were some men who passed their time as guests in shoemakers' shops, especially in winter;

their wives were fortunate in having other sources of income, and merely looked out for their rights in the matter of neighborhood news. These shoemakers' guests were a distinct and recognized class. There never were many of them, and they each had a sufficient excuse for idleness, either in their diligent wives, or some slight physical hindrance to active labor.

One cannot follow a farmer as he ploughs his furrows in a clayey field and expect the time to be given to steady conversation, but a shoemaker sits all day pounding, pegging, and silently shaping leather with his thin, sharp knife, at the receipt of custom and news. He likes to have his time beguiled with idle talk; he grows wise in many ways, and deeply reflective as he grows old. The humble hero of this brief tale, Mr. David Berry, was one of the pleasantest and wisest and least prejudiced of shoemakers. You could not spend five minutes' pegging time with him and miss hearing some ever-to-be-remembered piece of rural wisdom, some light coin of country speech, bearing the stamp of that mint where wit holds the hammer.

He was always an old-looking man for

his years, and as wise of countenance as a Greek philosopher. In the days when parishioners listened critically to sermons, and on Mondays and Tuesdays argued excitedly for and against the minister's opinions, Mr. David Berry, though never a fierce partisan, could always keep the points and heads of the discourses very clear in his mind. He was much respected among the old residents of the town, and always made Judge Hutton's and General Barstow's best boots, and patiently repaired the foot-gear of half the men and women of his neighborhood. Everything prospered with him in early life; his wife was busy and cheerful, and helped him to earn, though nobody could help him to save. His steady business brought in enough — Lynn work and custom work together — to pay for their house and a bit of land in course of time, but David Berry was one who liked to give for giving's sake; he believed with all his heart in foreign missions; he considered the poor, and was in every way a generous man. People did not notice this trait at first, because he never had large sums to give, and one never looked for his cramped handwriting at the head of a subscription paper, but you might always find it before you came to the end.

Everything prospered until he and his wife were far past middle life; then they suddenly became aware that the growth of the town was leaving them at one side. The tide of business had swept away from the old shoe shop. Sometimes Mr. Berry did not have a customer all day, and his wife came out with her sewing and sat on the doorstep to keep him company. The idlers had disappeared: some had gone to another world, and the rest evidently had followed the track of business; they were off at the square looking at men who drove new horses by, and tried to look unconscious; at mercantile strangers who came from Boston; at the great brick walls of the new mills which were going to bring so much money to the town. Professional idlers have no spirit of loyalty, they find occupation in the occupation of others, and they are fond of novelty.

Business had gone to another part of the town, and it was the plainest sort of good sense to follow it. One morning, after much trotting back and forward, an express wagon was backed up to the door of the little shoe shop in David Berry's yard, and loaded with the old shoe bench and the rusty stove, and all the sole-leather and old shoes and boots, and the idlers' chairs, and a great quantity of queer-shaped wooden lasts, and these were soon bestowed, looking meagre enough, in a narrow brick store down town. The rent had been a great lion in the way to a man who had never paid any rent; but Mrs. Berry was sanguine, and had no sentimental ties to the old shop, which she had always complained of as a dirty place and a temptation to the loafers of that neighborhood. Before long she succeeded in getting a good offer for the empty little building from a neighbor who was enlarging his hen house, and could not understand why her husband was slow to seize upon such a good handful of ready money, and even after he had taken it, would not stay at home and lend a hand at the moving. Mrs. Berry declared that the yard looked a great deal better without the old shoe shop. She could sit at her favorite window in the kitchen now, where the light was best, and look far down the street, as she never could before, to see the passing.

But David Berry felt old and bewildered

in his new quarters. The light was not nearly so good, and his tools were scattered, and he had to get up and cross the room half a dozen times in an hour, when formerly he had only to reach to the shelf above his head or across to the cutting board. He put up some signs in his window, made for him long ago out of friendship by one of the idlers, whose only gift was one for ornamental penmanship. "Boots and Shoes Repaired While You Wait" was the most prominent of these, and brought the industrious little man a good many hurried ten-cent jobs of pegging and heeling. Some of his old friends followed ·him; those who could afford to have their boots made still did so, for David Berry had won considerable renown for making comfortable shoes. But almost every one in the fast-growing, extravagant little town thought it better to spend two dollars three times in the six months than five dollars once, and ready-made boots and shoes were coming more and more into favor. Still there was work enough to do, though life was not half so friendly and pleasant as it used to be; and it always seemed strange to the little round-shouldered old man to take his long walk down the street after breakfast, and put the new key into the lock of an unfamiliar door. Mrs. Berry thought that her husband had lacked exercise, and that his walk did him good. She promoted him to a higher station of respectability in her own mind because he had a store down town, even though that store was a queer little three-cornered place tucked in at the head of the street between two large blocks.

There was only a north light in the new shop, and this seemed strange to a man who had been browned like a piece of the leather he worked upon because, small as the old shoe shop was, there were five windows in it, facing east and west and north, besides the upper half of the door, which was glazed, and faced to the southward. In dark weather, as the autumn came on, he had to light up early, and the care of the three lamps which were necessary for the new place of business seemed very troublesome. But he pegged and pounded away bravely. The old bench and the lapstone and all the tools were familiar, if the surroundings were not. He often said to himself that he should have felt like a king when he was a young journey-man to have had such a good location and outlook for business as this. There was an opportunity, besides, for making new friends. An old sailor with a wooden leg came in one morning to have his one boot patched, and the two men instantly recognized a capacity for comfortable companionship in one another. David Berry had made one wretched fishing voyage to the Banks before he finally settled upon his trade, and this made him a more intelligent listener to the life history of a mariner than was commonly to be found.

So the old sailor was unmolested in the best seat by the stove, by the time winter had set in. There was a poor little child, too, who came almost every day, and sat by the work-bench and watched the sharp knife and the round-headed hammer, the waxed ends and the lapstone, do their work. Mr. Berry had seen the little thing as he went to his work in the morning, and it being natural to him to inspect people's shoes before he glanced at their faces, he had been compassionate toward a worn-out sole, and offered his services at mending it. The child put her little hand into his, and they walked along together to the shop. She was a poor little body, and grateful for the luxurious warmth and for an apple, but the mended shoe she took quite as a matter of course. Ever since, she had come every day for a while, — to sit beside the bench, to run errands, to love the kind old man and look at him eagerly, — but into what crevice of the town she disappeared when she went out of the shop door, he never knew.

It came into Mr. David Berry's thoughts sometimes in the old shop how he had pegged away on his bench year after year, and how many men and women had kept him company for a time and then disappeared. There had been six ministers of the parish to which he and his wife belonged, and they had all gone away or died. It sometimes seemed as if he were going to peg away forever just the same, and the rest of the world change and change; but in these later days the world outside seemed to fare on its prosperous and unhindered way, while he was battling against change himself. But for all that, he liked many things in the new life. He was doing more business, if only the rent were not so high; and Mrs. Berry was completely satisfied with him, which was most delightful of all. She could not have treated him better if he had owned the whole new shoe factory that was just being fitted with its machinery and office furniture. Some misguided persons went so far as to suggest that David should apply for work there, but his wife was scornful in the extreme, and so, to tell the truth, was David himself. Since his days as apprentice, and a few months spent as a journeyman in seeing the shoemaking world, he had been his own man.

Some time went by, and business seemed just as good, and even the continuous stream of passers-by in the street made the old shoemaker feel as if he could not work fast enough to keep up with the times. There was no question among Mr. David Berry's friends about his unflagging prosperity. His friend the doctor, who said always and everywhere when he found opportunity that no shoemaker in town understood the anatomy of the human foot as Mr. Berry did, looked at him sharply once or twice, and asked if he got light enough, and if he had a good appetite nowadays, but there never was anything but an unaffectedly cheerful answer. The change had been good on the whole, and the rent was always paid on the day it was due, though Mrs. Berry forgot about it every quarter, and could not imagine what her man did with his money. Think of the work he had now! As much again as came to him in his shop in the yard. She asked him sometimes if he spent it for nuts and candy, remembering that in his early days he had yielded to such temptations, but David colored, and shook his head soberly. He did buy an apple or an orange for the little girl sometimes, but he could not confess it even to his wife. Mrs. Berry sometimes looked into the place of business, and once or twice had found the child there, and asked all sorts of questions, but the old man hastened to suggest another subject, saying that she did no mischief, and kept some others out of that chair who would be in it and bothering him if she were not. When the little clerk's mysterious grandmother kept her at home, Mr. Berry felt very lonely. She was an odd, silent child; but they felt the warmth of each other's affection without a word being said, and were contented in their opportunity of being together. Mr. Berry sometimes believed that if the grandmother should die, from whom this stray little person ran away daily, as a matter of course, he should try to persuade his wife to give the child a home.

Before long, Mrs. Berry would need some one to help in the house; but all this got no further than being a pleasant holiday flight of his imagination.

In the second year of Mr. David Berry's occupation of the down-town place of business he yielded to bad advice, and enlarged his business unguardedly. Sam Wescott, the man who had bought the old shoe shop, came in one night to get a pair of new boots, and after beating the price down unmercifully, and robbing honest David of nearly all his small profits, under pretense of hard times, and being a neighbor who had shown past favors about buying the building, he sat down for a friendly talk, saying that it was almost time for closing up, and then they could walk home together. David was glad to have a companion in his evening's journey of three quarters of a mile. He used to go home to dinner at first, but of late it seemed to keep him out of his shop just when the mill people were likely to wish to come in. The little girl was apt to come in at noon and share his feast.

"You 've got more room than you want here," said the unprofitable customer, looking about with a lordly air. "Why don't you put in some new stock? Why don't you keep ready-made boots?"

"I can't recommend them to customers," said the shoemaker, frowning.

"You need n't recommend them; they 'll be snapped up quick enough if you keep the prices low. Plenty of ways of getting round recommendations."

David Berry said nothing.

"And you are doing well as you are, so what you could sell extra would be clear gain, and draw in a sight o' folks who don't come now. I hear they sell second-choice shoes at the factory for next to nothing. My woman gets hers that way. You see, the thread 'll break, or the needle, and make a scratch on the leather, or there 'll be some little defect, and the shoe 's just as good to wear, but 't won't do to put in the shipping cases."

"I ain't goin' to palm off no such stuff on folks that respect either me or themselves," said Mr. David Berry, reddening.

"You can tell folks just what they be," urged the poultry merchant. "Some likes that kind the best. I can lend ye something to start on; just as soon lend ye as not."

The shoemaker rose and put by his tools

and his apron, but made no answer. The little girl, who was lingering late, waited until he had put on his coat and hat and locked the door, then put her hand into his and trotted at his side. Sam Wescott was amused at the sight, but after they passed two or three squares, the child slipped away silently down the side street.

" I 'd think the matter over about extending your business," he suggested again ; and this time David Berry said gravely that he would think of it, and ask Mrs. Berry ; then he spoke decidedly about other matters, but would hear no more of business until they parted.

He went in at the side door of his little house, and hung up his coat and hat in the narrow entry-way before he opened the door of the kitchen. Mrs. Berry was putting some old-fashioned shoe lasts into the stove. She was dressed all in her best, and there was a look of festivity ; it was evident that she had company to tea.

" Step into the bedroom quick as you can, David, an' put on a clean shirt and your best coat. Mis' Lester is here an' her son's wife. They come over from West Farms in the stage, shopping, and I over-persuaded 'em to spend the night. I just run over and asked the Wescotts to come too. I 've been wantin' to invite them this great while, you know; they 're some connection o' the Lesters. I can't make this fire burn, no matter what I do. Them lasts is got too old-fashioned even to burn."

"There, hold! hold!" exclaimed David, rescuing a treasure from the very jaws of the devouring stove. "That one ain't to be burnt; it 's a very particular last with me. I won't have ye take any o' those in the barrel."

"They 're all one to me," said Mrs. Berry, laughing. "I wish barrel and all was out o' my way. Come, go and dress up, David, and have some ambition besides hoardin' them old lasts!" She was very busy, but she turned round to look at him. "You feel well, don't you?" she asked anxiously, disturbed· by an unexplainable change in his looks. "Now you 're doin' so well, you might shut up shop for a week, and go off and have a good visit somewhere. I 'd like a change," she pleaded. "There, David Berry, you don't know how glad I be to have you out o' that little sixpenny shoe shop. I feel so free to have company when I want it, and not to stop and count every cent. I 'm going to make some o' my best tea-cakes, the kind that takes six eggs."

David stood, with the last in his hand, looking at her and faintly smiling approval. He was childishly delighted when she was pleased with herself and him, as she appeared to be to-night. Then he turned and went into the bedroom, and found his clean shirt and satin stock and Sunday coat spread out for him on the bed.

After tea was over, and the women had settled down to steady conversation, Sam Wescott returned to the subject of the extension of David Berry's capital, and David said that he had been thinking it over, and believed it would be no harm to try and work off a few dozen pairs of the factory shoes. He had put by something for a rainy day, though his rent hampered him all the time, and his wood bill had been double what he expected. There was no place to store firewood at the little shop, and he had to buy a foot at a time at an increased price. Before the tea party broke up, he had borrowed fifty dollars from Sam Wescott. There was nothing said about the interest not being put so high because they were neighbors. David Berry felt uneasy about this departure from his rule of never borrowing money, but he did n't like to touch what they had in the bank. It was little enough, and yet his wife really wanted to feel better off, now that she was in her prime. For himself, he was older, and would be contented to do without tea parties and the tea-cakes that took six eggs. But for several days Mrs. Berry kept saying, —

"What makes you so dumb, David?" And David would look at her with his slow smile, and make no excuse for himself.

A year went slowly by in these plain lives, and brought no change except that Mrs. Berry had a long siege of illness, and a woman had to be hired to take care of her, and the doctor's considerate bill was paid, and David Berry, that prudent, saving man, who had feared debt as if it were a tiger, found himself likely to be behindhand with his rent, and obliged for the first time to tell the parish collector that he could not pay the quarter's pew rent or his punctual missionary subscription until next month. The situation was not so terrible, after all, as he might have expected. His wife was slowly recovering her strength, and he had plenty of work to do. The little three-cornered shop was reopened, and he set himself to work again, and felt as prosperous as usual as soon as he felt the old hammer in his hand. The little girl was waiting about the door, though he had not been there for several weeks except for an hour or two at a time. He had forgotten his obligations to the business world in his cares of nursing and forlorn housekeeping; but now, as he assured the little clerk, for lack of a wiser confidante, he had found a good woman, who was glad to come and spend the rest of the winter. She looked at him wonderingly. It never occurred to him to persuade her into more confiding speech, because she always smiled at him when he looked up and smiled at her.

It is astonishing how one may feel secure in the presence of dreaded danger. David Berry became used to the surly calls of the rent agent and the wood and coal man, and to Sam Wescott's disagreeable references to the money that was still owed on account. David answered them all soberly that they must give him a little time. He had been in hard sledding lately, but was picking up his trade fast. The ready-made shoe business had not been successful, and while he was at home, a leak in the roof ruined the best of the stock, but he had managed to pay Sam Wescott all but sixteen dollars of the fifty. If it had not been his rule to pay the doctor's bill first after the minister's dues, he might have been ready with his rent. David Berry never was quick-handed; he was growing slower every year, and took great pains with his stitches and patches. At ten and fifteen cents each for his minor pieces of work, it took a good while to earn a dollar. "Give me a little time," he always said; "I mean to pay ye; I've always paid my bills, and asked no favors of any man until now." He worked as fast as he could and as long as he could, and spring was coming on; with the long days he could do even better.

One day, Sam Wescott, an impetuous, thoughtless sort of man, who liked to have his own way about things, and was rather fond of his petty grudges, met the rent collector of the property to which David Berry's place of business belonged.

"Can you get anything out of old Berry yet?" asked the rent collector.

"No, not yet; he keeps promising. I guess he'll pay, but I'm beginning to want my money," said Wescott pompously, as if he liked the reputation of having money out at interest.

" 'T ain't our rule to keep tenants who get behindhand," said the other. " He 's getting along in years, and all that. It ain't a shop that 's been called desirable heretofore, but there 's an Italian fellow after it sharp that wants to keep fruit, and I 've got to warn old Berry out, I guess, one o' these days."

Wescott ought to have been ashamed, but he really felt a lurking sense of satisfaction. The time had been when he had been in debt, not to say disgrace, which David Berry had taken occasion to justly comment upon, and the chance had now come to assist at David's own downfall. He might always have been steady at church, a good neighbor, and prompt of pay, and able to look every man in the face, but the welcome time had come to show him up as no better than other folks.

A few days afterward, the mischief having been set in motion, the blow fell out of a clear sky. The wood and coal man heard a whisper of other debts, and was quickly to the fore with his own account ; and the shoe-factory book-keeper sent an insolent young fellow to demand instant pay for the last purchase of shoes, although it wanted two weeks to the regular time of payment. Sam Wescott felt sorry when he slouched into the little shop and saw his old neighbor's scared, hurt, grayish face.   David Berry was keeping on with his work out of sheer force of habit. He did not know what his hands were doing; his honest heart grew duller and heavier every minute with pain.

"I was going to pay your bill to-morrow, sir," he said appealingly to the rent collector. "I thought that ought to come first. I 've been hard up for ready money, but I 've got within two dollars of it." He did not look at Sam Wescott.

"The rest of us has some rights," said the shoe-factory messenger loudly.

A crowd was gathering about the door; the poor little girl — the little clerk — began to cry. There were angry voices; somebody had brought a law paper. In a few minutes it was all over, like dying. David Berry had failed, and they were putting up his shutters.

When he fairly comprehended the great

blow, he stood up, swaying a little, just in front of the old shoe bench. "It ain't fair, neighbors," he said brokenly, — "it ain't fair. I had my rent 'most ready, and I don't owe Sam Wescott but sixteen dollars."

Then he burst into tears, — pleasant old David Berry, with his gray head and stooping shoulders, — and the little crowd ceased staring, and quickly disappeared, as if they felt a sense of shame.

"They say he owes everybody," one man told another contemptuously.

David Berry took his old hat at last, and stepped out of the door. The agent locked it, and took the key himself and put it into his pocket.

"I'll send up your things this afternoon, sir; the law can't touch a man's tools, you know," he said compassionately; but it was too late now for compassion to do David Berry any good. The old man walked feebly away, holding the ragged little girl by her thin hand.

Sam Wescott did not like the tone with which all his neighbors commented upon the news of Mr. Berry's failure. He explained carefully to every one that he felt sorry, but of course he had to put in his little bill with the rest. The whole sum of the old shoe-maker's indebtedness came to less than a hundred dollars.

All the neighbors and friends rallied to show their sympathy and good-will, but Mr. Berry did not have much to say. A look of patience under the blows of fate settled into his worn old face. He had his shoe bench put into the kitchen, and then wrote his name and occupation on a piece of paper, and tacked it to the gate. He sent away the woman who took care of his wife, though the good soul begged to stay, and he worked on and on from earliest morning to latest night. Presently his wife was about again, nervous and fretful, and ready to tiresomely deplore their altered fortunes to every customer. After the first influx of business prompted by sympathy, they seemed to be nearly forgotten again, and the old skilled workman bent his pride so low as to beg for work at the shoe factory, only to be contemptuously refused, simply because he was old.

Within a few months the doctor, who had been as kind as a brother to David Berry and his wife, met Sam Wescott going down the street, and with a set look in his kind face stopped his horse, and beckoned to the poultry merchant.

Sam stepped out to the roadside.

"I've just come from David Berry's," the doctor said; "and the good old man is going to die."

"What do you mean?" asked Sam, staring indignantly.

"He's going to die," repeated the doctor. "And I make no accusation, because I would rather believe you were thoughtless than malicious in shutting him up. But you might have fended off his troubles by a single word; you might have said you'd stand security for his rent. It broke his honest heart. You've seen yourself how he's grown twenty years older. You took away his pride, and you took away his living, and now he's got a touch of pneumonia, and is going as fast as he can go. I can't do anything for him; his vitality is all spent."

The doctor shook his reins and drove on, and Wescott went back to the sidewalk, very angry and somewhat dismayed. Nobody knew what made him so cross at home, especially on the day that David Berry died. The day of the funeral he pushed away from the gate a tearful little girl who stood there wistfully looking in. He muttered something about children being underfoot and staring at such times, and did not know that she was the silent little clerk, who had a perfect right to count herself among the mourners. She watched everybody go into the house and waited until they came out, and when the humble procession started, she walked beside it along the sidewalk, all the way to the burying-ground, as a faithful little dog might have done.

The next week somebody hung out a small red flag, and the neighbors gathered again to the auction. Mrs. Berry was broken in health, and every one said that it was best for her to sell the house, keeping some furniture for one room, and go up country to live with a cousin. Everything else was sold,—the best-room furniture (of which the good people had been so proud), the barrel of lasts, the lapstone and round hammer, the old shoe bench itself. David Berry was always slow and behind the times, many people said; he had been a good workman in his day, but he ran into debt and failed, and died; and his wife had broken up housekeeping and gone to live up country. Hardly any one remembered to say that he paid all his debts before he died, with interest, if there were any; the world could think of him only as a man that had failed in business.

Everybody missed him and his honest work unexpectedly, — the people who had been his near neighbors and received many kindnesses at his hands, whom he had watched with at night through their sicknesses and always been friendly with by day. Even strangers missed his kind face as he passed their houses.

One day Sam Wescott was standing in the old shoe shop, which made a little shed outside his poultry-yard, and he happened to notice a bit of printed paper pasted to the wall, low down, where it must have been close to the old shoe bench. He stooped to read it, out of curiosity, and found that it was only a verse out of the Bible: *Owe no man anything but to love one another.*

Sam Wescott looked at it again, then he walked away down the path with his hands behind him. In a minute or two he came back, took his jack-knife out of his pocket, and scratched the verse from the wall. Somehow there was no getting rid of one's thoughts about the old man. He had laughed once, and told somebody that David Berry could travel all day in a peck measure ; but now it seemed as if David Berry marched down upon him from the skies with a great army of those who owed no man anything but love, and had paid their debt.

THE PASSING OF SISTER BARSETT.

Mrs. Mercy Crane was of such firm
persuasion that a house is meant to be lived
in, that during many years she was never
known to leave her own neat two-storied
dwelling - place on the Ridge road.   Yet
being very fond of company, in pleasant
weather she often sat in the side doorway
looking out on her green yard, where the
grass grew short and thick and was undis-
figured even by a path toward the steps.
All her faded green blinds were securely
tied together and knotted on the inside by
pieces of white tape ; but now and then,
when the sun was not too hot for her
carpets, she opened one window at a time
for a few hours, having pronounced views
upon the necessity of light and air.   Although Mrs. Crane was acknowledged by
her best friends to be a peculiar person and
very set in her ways, she was much respected, and one acquaintance vied with
another in making up for her melancholy

seclusion by bringing her all the news they could gather. She had been left alone many years before by the sudden death of her husband from sunstroke, and though she was by no means poor, she had, as some one said, "such a pretty way of taking a little present that you could n't help being pleased when you gave her anything."

For a lover of society, such a life must have had its difficulties at times, except that the Ridge road was more traveled than any other in the township, and Mrs. Crane had invented a system of signals, to which she always resorted in case of wishing to speak to some one of her neighbors.

The afternoon was wearing late, one day toward the end of summer, and Mercy Crane sat in her doorway dressed in a favorite old-fashioned light calico and a small shoulder shawl figured with large palm leaves. She was making some tatting of a somewhat intricate pattern ; she believed it to be the prettiest and most durable of trimmings, and having decorated her own wardrobe in the course of unlimited leisure, she was now making a few yards apiece for each of her more intimate friends, so that they might have something to remember her by. She kept glancing up the road as if she expected some one, but the time went slowly by, until at last a woman appeared to view, walking fast, and carrying a large bundle in a checked handkerchief.

Then Mercy Crane worked steadily for a short time without looking up, until the desired friend was crossing the grass between the dusty road and the steps. The visitor was out of breath, and did not respond to the polite greeting of her hostess until she had recovered herself to her satisfaction. Mrs. Crane made her the kind offer of a glass of water or a few peppermints, but was answered only by a shake of the head, so she resumed her work for a time until the silence should be broken.

"I have come from the house of mourning," said Sarah Ellen Dow at last, unexpectedly.

"You don't tell me that Sister Barsett" —

"She's left us this time, she's really gone," and the excited news-bringer burst into tears. The poor soul was completely overwrought; she looked tired and wan, as if she had spent her forces in sympathy as well as hard work. She felt in her great bundle for a pocket handkerchief, but was not successful in the search, and finally produced a faded gingham apron with long, narrow strings, with which she hastily dried her tears. The sad news appealed also to Mercy Crane, who looked across to the apple-trees, and could not see them for a dazzle of tears in her own eyes. The spectacle of Sarah Ellen Dow going home with her humble workaday possessions, from the house where she had gone in haste only a few days before to care for a sick person well known to them both, was a very sad sight.

"You sent word yesterday that you should be returnin' early this afternoon, and would stop. I presume I received the message as you gave it?" asked Mrs. Crane, who was tenacious in such matters; "but I do declare I never looked to hear she was gone."

"She's been failin' right along sence yisterday about this time," said the nurse. "She's taken no notice to speak of, an' been eatin' the vally o' nothin', I may say, sence I went there a-Tuesday. Her sisters both come back yisterday, an' of course I was expected to give up charge to them.

They 're used to sickness, an' both havin' such a name for bein' great housekeepers!"

Sarah Ellen spoke with bitterness, but Mrs. Crane was reminded instantly of her own affairs. "I feel condemned that I ain't begun my own fall cleanin' yet," she said, with an ostentatious sigh.

"Plenty o' time to worry about that," her friend hastened to console her.

"I do desire to have everything decent about my house," resumed Mrs. Crane. "There 's nobody to do anything but me. If I was to be taken away sudden myself, I should n't want to have it said afterwards that there was wisps under my sofy or — There! I can't dwell on my own troubles with Sister Barsett's loss right before me. I can't seem to believe she 's really passed away; she always was saying she should go in some o' these spells, but I deemed her to be troubled with narves."

Sarah Ellen Dow shook her head. "I 'm all nerved up myself," she said brokenly. "I made light of her sickness when I went there first, I 'd seen her what she called dreadful low so many times; but I saw her looks this morning, an' I begun to believe her at last. Them sisters o' hers is the master for unfeelin' hearts.   Sister Barsett was a-layin' there yisterday, an' one of 'em was a-settin' right by her tellin' how diffi-cult 't was for her to leave home, her niece was goin' to graduate to the high school, an' they was goin' to have a time in the evening, an' all the exercises promised to be extry interesting.   Poor Sister Barsett knew what she said an' looked at her with contempt, an' then she give a glance at me an' closed up her eyes as if 't was for the last time.   I know she felt it."

Sarah Ellen Dow was more and more ex-cited by a sense of bitter grievance.   Her rule of the afflicted household had evidently been interfered with; she was not accustomed to be ignored and set aside at such times. Her simple nature and uncommon ability found satisfaction in the exercise of authority, but she had now left her post feeling hurt and wronged, besides knowing something of the pain of honest affliction.

"If it had n't been for esteemin' Sister Barsett as I always have done, I should have told 'em no, an' held to it, when they asked me to come back an' watch to-night.   'T ain't for none o' their sakes, but Sister Barsett was a good friend to me in her way."   Sarah

Ellen broke down once more, and felt in her bundle again hastily, but the handkerchief was again elusive, while a small object fell out upon the doorstep with a bounce.

" 'T ain't nothin' but a little taste-cake I spared out o' the loaf I baked this mornin'," she explained, with a blush. " I was so shoved out that I seemed to want to turn my hand to somethin' useful an' feel I was still doin' for Sister Barsett. Try a little piece, won't you, Mis' Crane? I thought it seemed light an' good."

They shared the taste-cake with serious enjoyment, and pronounced it very good indeed when they had finished and shaken the crumbs out of their laps. " There 's nobody but you shall come an' do for me at the last, if I can have my way about things," said Mercy Crane impulsively. She meant it for a tribute to Miss Dow's character and general ability, and as such it was meekly accepted.

" You 're a younger person than I be, an' less wore," said Sarah Ellen, but she felt better now that she had rested, and her conversational powers seemed to be refreshed by her share of the little cake. " Doctor Bangs has behaved real pretty, I can say that," she continued presently in a mournful tone.

"Heretofore, in the sickness of Sister Barsett, I have always felt to hope certain that she would survive; she's recovered from a sight o' things in her day. She has been the first to have all the new diseases that's visited this region. I know she had the spinal mergeetis months before there was any other case about," observed Mrs. Crane with satisfaction.

"An' the new throat troubles, all of 'em," agreed Sarah Ellen; "an' has made trial of all the best patent medicines, an' could tell you their merits as no one else could in this vicinity. She never was one that depended on herbs alone, though she considered 'em extremely useful in some cases. Everybody has their herb, as we know, but I'm free to say that Sister Barsett sometimes done everything she could to kill herself with such rovin' ways o' dosin'. She must see it now she's gone an' can't stuff down no more invigorators." Sarah Ellen Dow burst out suddenly with this, as if she could no longer contain her honest opinion.

"There, there! you're all worked up," answered placid Mercy Crane, looking more interested than ever.

"An' she was dreadful handy to talk religion to other folks, but I 've come to a realizin' sense that religion is somethin' besides opinions. She an' Elder French has been mostly of one mind, but I don't know's they 've got hold of all the religion there is."

"Why, why, Sarah Ellen!" exclaimed Mrs. Crane, but there was still something in her tone that urged the speaker to further expression of her feelings. The good creature was much excited, her face was clouded with disapproval.

"I ain't forgettin' nothin' about their good points either," she went on in a more subdued tone, and suddenly stopped.

"Preachin' 'll be done away with soon or late, — preachin' o' Elder French's kind," announced Mercy Crane, after waiting to see if her guest did not mean to say anything more. "I should like to read 'em out that verse another fashion : 'Be ye doers o' the word, not preachers only,' would hit it about right; but there, it 's easy for all of us to talk. In my early days I used to like to get out to meetin' regular, because sure as I did n't I had bad luck all the week. I did n't feel pacified 'less I 'd been half a day, but I was out all day the Sabbath before Mr. Barlow died as he did. So you mean to say that Sister Barsett's really gone?"

Mrs. Crane's tone changed to one of real concern, and her manner indicated that she had put the preceding conversation behind her with decision.

"She was herself to the last," instantly responded Miss Dow. "I see her put out a thumb an' finger from under the spread an' pinch up a fold of her sister Deckett's dress, to try an' see if 't was all wool. I thought 't wa'n't all wool, myself, an' I know it now by the way she looked. She was a very knowin' person about materials; we shall miss poor Mis' Barsett in many ways, she was always the one to consult with about matters o' dress."

"She passed away easy at the last, I hope?" asked Mrs. Crane with interest.

"Why, I wa'n't there, if you'll believe it!" exclaimed Sarah Ellen, flushing, and looking at her friend for sympathy. "Sister Barsett revived up the first o' the afternoon, an' they sent for Elder French. She took notice of him, and he exhorted quite a spell, an' then he spoke o' there being need of air in the room, Mis' Deckett havin' closed every window, an' she asked me of all folks if I had n't better step out; but Elder French come too, an' he was very reasonable, an' had a word with me about Mis' Deckett an' Mis' Peak an' the way they was workin' things. I told him right out how they never come near when the rest of us was havin' it so hard with her along in the spring, but now they thought she was re'lly goin' to die, they come settlin' down like a pair o' old crows in a field to pick for what they could get. I just made up my mind they should have all the care if they wanted it. It did n't seem as if there was anything more I could do for Sister Barsett, an' I set there in the kitchen within call an' waited, an' when I heard 'em sayin', ' There, she 's gone, she 's gone ! ' and Mis' Deckett a-weepin', I put on my bunnit and stepped myself out into the road. I felt to repent after I had gone but a rod, but I was so worked up, an' I thought they 'd call me back, an' then I was put out because they did n't, an' so here I be. I can't help it now." Sarah Ellen was crying again ; she and Mrs. Crane could not look at each other.

" Well, you set an' rest," said Mrs. Crane kindly, and with the merest shadow of disapproval. "You set an' rest, an' by an' by, if you 'd feel better, you could go back an' just make a little stop an' inquire about the arrangements. I would n't harbor no feelin's, if they be inconsiderate folks. Sister Barsett has often deplored their actions in my hearing an' wished she had sisters like other folks. With all her faults she was a useful person an' a good neighbor," mourned Mercy Crane sincerely. "She was one that always had somethin' interestin' to tell, an' if it wa'n't for her dyin' spells an' all that sort o' nonsense, she 'd make a figger in the world, she would so. She walked with an air always, Mis' Barsett did ; you 'd ask who she was if you had n't known, as she passed you by. How quick we forget the outs about anybody that 's gone ! but I always feel grateful to anybody that 's friendly, situated as I be. I shall miss her runnin' over. I can seem to see her now, coming over the rise in the road. But don't you get in a way of takin' things too hard, Sarah Ellen ! You 've worked yourself all to pieces since I saw you last ; you 're gettin' to be as lean as a meetin'-house fly. Now, you 're comin' in to have a cup o' tea with me, an' then you 'll feel better. I 've got some new molasses gingerbread that I baked this mornin'."

"I do feel beat out, Mis' Crane," acknow-ledged the poor little soul, glad of a chance to speak, but touched by this unexpected mark of consideration. "If I could ha' done as I wanted to I should be feelin' well enough, but to be set aside an' ordered about, where I 'd taken the lead in sickness so much, an' knew how to deal with Sister Barsett so well! She might be livin' now, perhaps" —

"Come ; we 'd better go in, 't is gettin' damp," and the mistress of the house rose so hurriedly as to seem bustling. "Don't dwell on Sister Barsett an' her foolish folks no more ; I would n't, if I was you."

They went into the front room, which was dim with the twilight of the half-closed blinds and two great syringa bushes that grew against them. Sarah Ellen put down her bundle and bestowed herself in the large, cane-seated rocking-chair. Mrs. Crane di-rected her to stay there awhile and rest, and then come out into the kitchen when she got ready.

A cheerful clatter of dishes was heard at once upon Mrs. Crane's disappearance. "I hope she 's goin' to make one o' her nice short-cakes, but I don't know 's she 'll think it quite worth while," thought the guest humbly.   She desired to go out into the kitchen, but it was proper behavior to wait until she should be called.   Mercy Crane was not a person with whom one could venture to take liberties.   Presently Sarah Ellen began to feel better.   She did not often find such a quiet place, or the quarter of an hour of idleness in which to enjoy it, and was glad to make the most of this opportunity.   Just now she felt tired and lonely.   She was a busy, unselfish, eager - minded creature by nature, but now, while grief was sometimes uppermost in her mind and sometimes a sense of wrong, every moment found her more peaceful, and the great excitement little by little faded away.

" What a person poor Sister Barsett was to dread growing old so she could n't get about.   I 'm sure I shall miss her as much as anybody," said Mrs. Crane, suddenly opening the kitchen door, and letting in an unmistakable and delicious odor of short-cake that revived still more the drooping spirits of her guest.   " An' a good deal of knowledge has died with her," she added, coming into the room and seeming to make it lighter.

" There, she knew a good deal, but she

did n't know all, especially o' doctorin'," insisted Sarah Ellen from the rocking-chair, with an unexpected little laugh. " She used to lay down the law to me as if I had neither sense nor experience, but when it came to her bad spells she 'd always send for me. It takes everybody to know everything, but Sister Barsett was of an opinion that her information was sufficient for the town. She was tellin' me the day I went there how she disliked to have old Mis' Doubleday come an' visit with her, an' remarked that she called Mis' Doubleday very officious. ' Went right down on her knees an' prayed,' says she. ' Anybody would have thought I was a heathen ! ' But I kind of pacified her feelin's, an' told her I supposed the old lady meant well."

" Did she give away any of her things? — Mis' Barsett, I mean," inquired Mrs. Crane.

" Not in my hearin'," replied Sarah Ellen Dow. " Except one day, the first of the week, she told her oldest sister, Mis' Deckett, — 't was that first day she rode over, — that she might have her green quilted petticoat ; you see it was a rainy day, an' Mis' Deckett had complained o' feelin' thin. She went right up an' got it, and put it on an' wore it off, an' I 'm sure I thought no more about it, until I heard Sister Barsett groanin' dreadful in the night. I got right up to see what the matter was, an' what do you think but she was wantin' that petticoat back, and not thinking any too well o' Nancy Deckett for takin' it when 't was offered. 'Nancy never showed no sense o' propriety,' says Sister Barsett; I just wish you 'd heard her go on!

"If she had felt to remember me," continued Sarah Ellen, after they had laughed a little, "I 'd full as soon have some of her nice crockery-ware. She told me once, years ago, when I was stoppin' to tea with her an' we were havin' it real friendly, that she should leave me her Britannia tea-set, but I ain't got it in writin', and I can't say she 's ever referred to the matter since. It ain't as if I had a home o' my own to keep it in, but I should have thought a great deal of it for her sake," and the speaker's voice faltered. "I must say that with all her virtues she never was a first-class housekeeper, but I would n't say it to any but a friend. You never eat no preserves o' hers that wa'n't commencin' to work, an' you know as well as I how little forethought she had about putting away her woolens. I sat behind her once in meetin' when I was stoppin' with the Tremletts and so occupied a seat in their pew, an' I see between ten an' a dozen moth millers come workin' out o' her fitch-fur tippet. They was flutterin' round her bonnet same 's 't was a lamp. I should be mortified to death to have such a thing happen to me."

" Every housekeeper has her weak point; I 've got mine as much as anybody else," acknowledged Mercy Crane with spirit, " but you never see no moth millers come workin' out o' me in a public place."

"Ain't your oven beginning to get over-het?" anxiously inquired Sarah Ellen Dow, who was sitting more in the draught, and could not bear to have any accident happen to the supper. Mrs. Crane flew to a shortcake's rescue, and presently called her guest to the table.

The two women sat down to deep and brimming cups of tea. Sarah Ellen noticed with great gratification that her hostess had put on two of the best tea-cups and some citron-melon preserves. It was not an every-day supper. She was used to hard fare, poor, hard-working Sarah Ellen, and this handsome social attention did her good. Sister Crane rarely entertained a friend, and it would be a pleasure to speak of the tea-drinking for weeks to come.

"You 've put yourself out quite a consid'able for me," she acknowledged. "How pretty these cups is! You ought n't to use 'em so common as for me. I wish I had a home I could really call my own to ask you to, but 't ain't never been so I could. Sometimes I wonder what 's goin' to become o' me when I get so I 'm past work. Takin' care o' sick folks an' bein' in houses where there 's a sight goin' on an' everybody in a hurry kind of wears on me now I 'm most a-gittin' in years. I was wishin' the other day that I could get with some comfortable kind of a sick person, where I could live right along quiet as other folks do, but folks never sends for me 'less they 're drove to it. I ain't laid up anything to really depend upon."

The situation appealed to Mercy Crane, well to do as she was and not burdened with responsibilities. She stirred uneasily in her chair, but could not bring herself to the point of offering Sarah Ellen the home she coveted.

"Have some hot tea," she insisted, in a matter of fact tone, and Sarah Ellen's face, which had been lighted by a sudden eager hopefulness, grew dull and narrow again.

"Plenty, plenty, Mis' Crane," she said sadly, "'t is beautiful tea, — you always have good tea;" but she could not turn her thoughts from her own uncertain future. "None of our folks has ever lived to be a burden," she said presently, in a pathetic tone, putting down her cup. "My mother was thought to be doing well until four o'clock an' was dead at ten. My Aunt Nancy came to our house well at twelve o'clock an' died that afternoon; my father was sick but ten days. There was dear sister Betsy, she did go in consumption, but 't wa'n't an expensive sickness."

"I 've thought sometimes about you, how you 'd get past rovin' from house to house one o' these days. I guess your friends will stand by you." Mrs. Crane spoke with unwonted sympathy, and Sarah Ellen's heart leaped with joy.

"You 're real kind," she said simply. "There 's nobody I set so much by. But I shall miss Sister Barsett, when all 's said an' done. She 's asked me many a time to stop with her when I was n't doin' nothin'. We all have our failin's, but she was a friendly creatur'. I sha'n't want to see her laid away."

"Yes, I was thinkin' a few minutes ago that I should n't want to look out an' see the funeral go by. She 's one o' the old neighbors. I s'pose I shall have to look, or I should n't feel right afterward," said Mrs. Crane mournfully. "If I had n't got so kind of housebound," she added with touching frankness, "I 'd just as soon go over with you an' offer to watch this night."

"'T would astonish Sister Barsett so I don't know but she 'd return." Sarah Ellen's eyes danced with amusement; she could not resist her own joke, and Mercy Crane herself had to smile.

"Now I must be goin', or 't will be dark," said the guest, rising and sighing after she had eaten her last crumb of gingerbread. "Yes, thank ye, you 're real good, I will come back if I find I ain't wanted. Look what a pretty sky there is!" and the two friends went to the side door and stood together in a moment of affectionate silence, looking out toward the sunset across the wide fields. The country was still with that deep rural stillness which seems to mean the absence of humanity. Only the thrushes were singing far away in the walnut woods beyond the orchard, and some crows were flying over and cawed once loudly, as if they were speaking to the women at the door.

Just as the friends were parting, after most grateful acknowledgments from Sarah Ellen Dow, some one came driving along the road in a hurry and stopped.

"Who's that with you, Mis' Crane?" called one of their near neighbors.

"It's Sarah Ellen Dow," answered Mrs.. Crane. "What's the matter?"

"I thought so, but I could n't rightly see. Come, they are in a peck o' trouble up to Sister Barsett's, wonderin' where you be," grumbled the man. "They can't do nothin' with her; she's drove off everybody an' keeps a-screechin' for you. Come, step along, Sarah Ellen, do!"

"Sister Barsett!" exclaimed both the women. Mercy Crane sank down upon the doorstep, but Sarah Ellen stepped out upon the grass all of a tremble, and went toward the wagon. "They said this afternoon that Sister Barsett was gone," she managed to say. "What did they mean?"

"Gone where?" asked the impatient neighbor. "I expect 't was one of her spells. She 's come to; they say she wants somethin' hearty for her tea. Nobody can't take one step till you get there, neither."

Sarah Ellen was still dazed; she returned to the doorway, where Mercy Crane sat shaking with laughter. "I don't know but we might as well laugh as cry," she said in an aimless sort of way. "I know you too well to think you 're going to repeat a single word. Well, I 'll get my bonnet an' start; ·I expect I 've got considerable to cope with, but I 'm well rested. Good-night, Mis' Crane, I certain did have a beautiful tea, whatever the future may have in store."

She wore a solemn expression as she mounted into the wagon in haste and departed, but she was far out of sight when Mercy Crane stopped laughing and went into the house.

MISS ESTHER'S GUEST.

I.

Old Miss Porley put on her silk shawl, and arranged it carefully over her thin shoulders, and pinned it with a hand that shook a little as if she were much excited. She bent forward to examine the shawl in the mahogany-framed mirror, for there was a frayed and tender spot in the silk where she had pinned it so many years. The shawl was very old; it had been her mother's, and she disliked to wear it too often, but she never could make up her mind to go out into the street in summer, as some of her neighbors did, with nothing over her shoulders at all. Next she put on her bonnet and tried to set it straight, allowing for a wave in the looking-glass that made one side of her face appear much longer than the other; then she drew on a pair of well-darned silk gloves; one had a wide crack all the way up the back of the hand, but they were still neat

and decent for every-day wear, if she were
careful to keep her left hand under the edge
of the shawl. She had discussed the propriety of drawing the raveled silk together,
but a thick seam would look very ugly, and
there was something accidental about the
crack.

Then, after hesitating a few moments, she
took a small piece of folded white letter-
paper from the table and went out of the
house, locking the door and trying it, and
stepped away bravely down the village street.
Everybody said, "How do you do, Miss
Porley?" or "Good-mornin', Esther." Every
one in Daleham knew the good woman; she
was one of the unchanging persons, always
to be found in her place, and always pleased
and friendly and ready to take an interest
in old and young. She and her mother,
who had early been left a widow, had been
for many years the village tailoresses and
makers of little boys' clothes. Mrs. Porley
had been dead three years, however, and
her daughter "Easter," as old friends called
our heroine, had lived quite alone. She
was made very sorrowful by her loneliness,
but she never could be persuaded to take
anybody to board : she could not bear

to think of any one's taking her mother's place.

It was a warm summer morning, and Miss Porley had not very far to walk, but she was still more shaky and excited by the time she reached the First Church parsonage. She stood at the gate undecidedly, and, after she pushed it open a little way, she drew back again, and felt a curious beating at her heart and a general reluctance of mind and body. At that moment the minister's wife, a pleasant young woman with a smiling, eager face, looked out of the window and asked the tremulous visitor to come in. Miss Esther straightened herself and went briskly up the walk; she was very fond of the minister's wife, who had only been in Daleham a few months.

"Won't you take off your shawl?" asked Mrs. Wayton affectionately; "I have just been making gingerbread, and you shall have a piece as soon as it cools."

"I don't know 's I ought to stop," answered Miss Esther, flushing quickly. "I came on business; I won't keep you long."

"Oh, please stay a little while," urged the hostess. "I 'll take my sewing, if you don't mind; there are two or three things that I want to ask you about."

"I've thought and flustered a sight over taking this step," said good old Esther abruptly. "I had to conquer a sight o' reluctance, I must say. I've got so used to livin' by myself that I sha'n't know how to consider another. But I see I ain't got common feelin' for others unless I can set my own comfort aside once in a while. I've brought you my name as one of those that will take one o' them city folks that needs a spell o' change. It come straight home to me how I should be feeling it by this time, if my lot had been cast in one o' them city garrets that the minister described so affecting. If 't had n't been for kind consideration somewheres, mother an' me might have sewed all them pleasant years away in the city that we enjoyed so in our own home, and our garding to step right out into when our sides set in to ache. And I ain't rich, but we was able to save a little something, and now I'm eatin' of it all up alone. It come to me I should like to have somebody take a taste out o' mother's part. Now, don't you let 'em send me no rampin' boys like them Barnard's folks had come last year, that vexed dumb creatur's so; and I don't know how to cope with no kind o'

men-folks or strange girls, but I should
know how to do for a woman that 's getting well along in years, an' has come to feel
kind o' spent. P'raps we ain't no right to
pick an' choose, but I should know best how
to make that sort comfortable on 'count of
doin' for mother and studying what she
preferred."

Miss Esther rose with quaint formality
and put the folded paper, on which she had
neatly written her name and address, into
Mrs. Wayton's hand. Mrs. Wayton rose
soberly to receive it, and then they both sat
down again.

" I 'm sure that you will feel more than re-
paid for your kindness, dear Miss Esther,"
said the minister's wife. " I know one of the
ladies who have charge of the arrangements
for the Country Week, and I will explain
as well as I can the kind of guest you have
in mind. I quite envy her : I have often
thought, when I was busy and tired, how
much I should like to run along the street
and make you a visit in your dear old-fashioned little house."

"I should be more than pleased to have
you, I 'm sure," said Miss Esther, startled
into a bright smile and forgetting her anx-

iety. "Come any day, and take me just as I am. We used to have a good deal o' company years ago, when there was a number o' mother's folks still livin' over Ashfield way. Sure as we had a pile o' work on hand and was hurrying for dear life an' limb, a wagon-load would light down at the front gate to spend the day an' have an early tea. Mother never was one to get flustered same 's I do 'bout everything. She was a lovely cook, and she 'd fill 'em up. an' cheer 'em, and git 'em off early as she could, an' then we 'd be kind o' waked up an' spirited our-selves, and would set up late sewin' and talkin' the company over, an' I 'd have things saved to tell her that had been said while she was out o' the room. I make such a towse over everything myself, but mother was waked right up and felt pleased an' smart, if anything unexpected happened. I miss her more every year," and Miss Esther gave a great sigh. "I s'pose 't wa'n't reasonable to expect that I could have her to help me through with old age, but I 'm a poor tool, alone."

"Oh, no, you must n't say that!" ex-claimed the minister's wife. "Why, nobody could get along without you. I wish I had come to Daleham in time to know your mother too."

Miss Esther shook her head sadly. "She would have set everything by you and Mr. Wayton. Now I must be getting back in case I'm wanted, but you let 'em send me somebody right away, while my bush beans is so nice. An' if any o' your little boy's clothes wants repairin', just give 'em to me; 't will be a real pleasant thing to set a few stitches. Or the minister's; ain't there something needed for him?"

Mrs. Wayton was about to say no, when she became conscious of the pleading old face before her. "I'm sure you are most kind, dear friend," she answered, "and I do have a great deal to do. I'll bring you two or three things to-night that are beyond my art, as I go to evening meeting. Mr. Wayton frayed out his best coat sleeve yesterday, and I was disheartened, for we had counted upon his not having a new one before the fall."

" 'T would be mere play to me," said Miss Esther, and presently she went smiling down the street.

II.

The Committee for the Country Week in a certain ward of Boston were considering the long list of children, and mothers with babies, and sewing-women, who were looking forward, some of them for the first time in many years, to a country holiday. Some were to go as guests to hospitable, generous farmhouses that opened their doors willingly now and then to tired city people; for some persons board could be paid.

The immediate arrangements of that time were settled at last, except that Mrs. Belton, the chairman, suddenly took a letter from her pocket. "I had almost forgotten this," she said; " it is another place offered in dear quiet old Daleham. My friend, the minister's wife there, writes me a word about it: ' The applicant desires especially an old person, being used to the care of an aged parent and sure of her power of making such a one comfortable, and she would like to have her guest come as soon as possible.' My friend asks me to choose a person of some refinement, — ' one who would appreciate the delicate simplicity and quaint ways of the hostess.' "

Mrs. Belton glanced hurriedly down the page. " I believe that's all," she said. " How about that nice old sewing-woman, Mrs. Connolly, in Bantry Street ? "

" Oh, no ! " some one entreated, looking up from her writing. " Why is n't it just the place for my old Mr. Rill, the dear old Englishman who lives alone up four flights in Town Court and has the bullfinch. He used to engrave seals, and his eyes gave out, and he is so thrifty with his own bit of savings and an atom of a pension. Some one pays his expenses to the country, and this sounds like a place he would be sure to like. I 've been watching for the right chance."

" Take it, then," said the busy chairman, and there was a little more writing and talking, and then the committee meeting was over which settled Miss Esther Porley's fate.

III.

The journey to Daleham was a great experience to Mr. Rill. He was a sensible old person, who knew well that he was getting stiffer and clumsier than need be in his garret, and that, as certain friends had said, a short time spent in the country would cheer and invigorate him. There had been occasional propositions that he should leave his garret altogether and go to the country to live, or at least to the suburbs of the city. He could not see things close at hand so well as he could take a wide outlook, and as his outlook from the one garret window was a still higher brick wall and many chimneys, he was losing a great deal that he might have had. But so long as he was expected to take an interest in the unseen and unknown he failed to accede to any plans about the country home, and declared that he was well enough in his high abode. He had lost a sister a few years before who had been his mainstay, but with his hands so well used to delicate work he had been less bungling in his simple household affairs than many another man might have been. But he was very lonely and was growing anxious; as he was rattled along in the train toward Daleham he held the chirping bullfinch's cage fast with both hands, and said to himself now and then, " This may lead to something; the country air smells very good to me."

The Daleham station was not very far out of the village, so that Miss Esther Porley put on her silk shawl and bonnet and every-day gloves just before four o'clock that afternoon, and went to meet her Country Week guest. Word had come the day before that the person for Miss Porley's would start two days in advance of the little company of children and helpless women, and since this message had come from the parsonage Miss Esther had worked diligently, late and early, to have her house in proper order. Whatever her mother had liked was thought of and provided. There were going to be rye short-cakes for tea, and there were some sprigs of thyme and sweet-balm in an old-fashioned wine-glass on the keeping-room table; mother always said they were so freshening. And Miss Esther had taken out a little shoulder-shawl and folded it over the arm of the rock-ing - chair by the window that looked out into the small garden where the London-pride was in full bloom, and the morning-glories had just begun to climb. Miss Esther was sixty-four herself, but still looked upon age as well in the distance.

She was always a prompt person, and had some minutes to wait at the station; then the time passed and the train was late. At last she saw the smoke far in the distance, and her heart began to sink. Perhaps she would not find it easy to get on with the old lady, and — well it was only for a week, and she had thought it right and best to take such a step, and now it would soon be over.

The train stopped, and there was no old lady at all.

Miss Esther had stood far back to get away from the smoke and roar, — she was always as afraid of the cars as she could be, — but as they moved away she took a few steps forward to scan the platform. There was no black bonnet with a worn lace veil, and no old lady with a burden of bundles ; there were only the station master and two or three men, and an idle boy or two, and one clean-faced, bent old man with a bird-cage in one hand and an old carpet-bag in the other. She thought of the rye short-cakes for supper and all that she had done to make her small home pleasant, and her fire of excitement suddenly fell into ashes.

The old man with the bird-cage suddenly turned toward her. "Can you direct me to Miss Esther Porley's ? " said he.

"I can," replied Miss Esther, looking at him with curiosity.

"I was directed to her house," said the

pleasant old fellow, " by Mrs. Belton, of the Country Week Committee. My eyesight is poor. I should be glad if anybody would help me to find the place."

"You step this way with me, sir," said Miss Esther. She was afraid that the men on the platform heard every word they said, but nobody took particular notice, and off they walked down the road together. Miss Esther was enraged with the Country Week Committee.

" *You* were sent to — Miss Porley's ? " she asked grimly, turning to look at him.

" I was, indeed," said Mr. Rill.

" I am Miss Porley, and I expected an old lady," she managed to say, and they both stopped and looked at each other with apprehension.

" I do declare ! " faltered the old seal-cutter anxiously. " What had I better do, ma'am? They most certain give me your name. May be you could recommend me somewheres else, an' I can get home to-morrow if 't ain't convenient."

They were standing under a willow-tree in the shade ; Mr. Rill took off his heavy hat, — it was a silk hat of by-gone shape ; a golden robin began to sing, high in the willow, and the old bullfinch twittered and chirped in the cage. Miss Esther heard some footsteps coming behind them along the road. She changed color; she tried to remember that she was a woman of mature years and considerable experience.

"'T ain't a mite o' matter, sir," she said cheerfully. "I guess you 'll find everything comfortable for you;" and they turned, much relieved, and walked along together.

"That 's Lawyer Barstow's house," she said calmly, a minute afterward, "the handsomest place in town, we think 't is," and Mr. Rill answered politely that Daleham was a pretty place; he had not been out of the city for so many years that everything looked beautiful as a picture.

IV.

Miss Porley rapidly recovered her composure, and bent her energies to the preparing of an early tea. She showed her guest to the snug bedroom under the low gambrel roof, and when she apologized for his having to go upstairs, he begged her to remember that it was nothing but a step to a man who was used to four long flights. They were both excited at finding a proper nail for the birdcage outside the window, though Miss Esther said that she should love to have the pretty bird downstairs where they could see it and hear it sing. She said to herself over and over that if she could have her long-lost brother come home from sea, she should like to have him look and behave as gentle and kind as Mr. Rill. Somehow she found herself singing a cheerful hymn as she mixed and stirred the short-cakes. She could not help wishing that her mother were there to enjoy this surprise, but it did seem very odd, after so many years, to have a man in the house. It had not happened for fifteen years, at least, when they had entertained Deacon Sparks and wife, delegates from the neighboring town of East Wilby to the County Conference.

The neighbors did not laugh at Miss Esther openly or cause her to blush with self-consciousness, however much they may have discussed the situation and smiled behind her back. She took the presence of her guest with delighted simplicity, and the country week was extended to a fortnight, and then to a month. At last, one day Miss

Esther and Mr. Rill were seen on their way to the railroad station, with a large bundle apiece beside the carpet-bag, though some one noticed that the bullfinch was left behind. Miss Esther came back alone, looking very woebegone and lonely, and if the truth must be known, she found her house too solitary. She looked into the woodhouse where there was a great store of kindlings, neatly piled, and her water-pail was filled to the brim, her garden-paths were clean of weeds and swept, and yet everywhere she looked it seemed more lonely than ever. She pinned on her shawl again and went along the street to the parsonage.

"My old lady's just gone," she said to the minister's wife. "I was so lonesome I could not stay in the house."

"You found him a very pleasant visitor, did n't you, Miss Esther?" asked Mrs. Wayton, laughing a little.

"I did so; he wa'n't like other men,—kind and friendly and fatherly, and never stayed round when I was occupied, but entertained himself down street considerable, an' was as industrious as a bee, always asking me if there wa'n't something he could do about house. He and a sister some years older

used to keep house together, and it was her
long sickness used up what they 'd saved,
and yet he 's got a little somethin', and there
are friends he used to work for, jewelers, a
big firm, that gives him somethin' regular.
He 's goin' to see,"—and Miss Esther blushed
crimson, — " he 's goin' to see if they 'd be
willin' to pay it just the same if he come to
reside in Daleham. He thinks the air agrees
with him here."

" Does he indeed ? " inquired the minister's
wife, with deep interest and a look of amusement.

" Yes 'm," said Miss Esther simply ; " but
don't you go an' say nothin' yet. I don't
want folks to make a joke of it. Seems to
me if he does feel to come back, and remains
of the same mind he went away, we might be
judicious to take the step " —

" Why, Miss Esther ! " exclaimed the listener.

" Not till fall, — not till fall," said Miss
Esther hastily. " I ain't going to count on
it too much anyway. I expect we could get
along ; there 's considerable goodness left in
me, and you can always work better when
you 've got somebody beside yourself to work
for. There, now I 've told you I feel as if
I was blown away in a gale."

" Why, I don't know what to say at such a piece of news! " exclaimed Mrs. Wayton again.

" I don't know 's there 's anything *to* say," gravely answered Miss Esther. " But I did laugh just now coming in the gate to think what a twitter I got into the day I fetched you that piece of paper."

" Why, I must go right and tell Mr. Wayton! " said the minister's wife.

" Oh, don't you, Mis' Wayton ; no, no! " begged Miss Esther, looking quite coy and girlish. " I really don't know 's it 's quite settled, — it don't seem 's if it could be. I 'm going to hear from him in the course of a week. But I suppose *he* thinks it 's settled ; he 's left the bird."

THE FLIGHT OF BETSEY LANE.

I.

ONE windy morning in May, three old women sat together near an open window in the shed chamber of Byfleet Poor-house. The wind was from the northwest, but their window faced the southeast, and they were only visited by an occasional pleasant waft of fresh air. They were close together, knee to knee, picking over a bushel of beans, and commanding a view of the dandelion-starred, green yard below, and of the winding, sandy road that led to the village, two miles away. Some captive bees were scolding among the cobwebs of the rafters overhead, or thumping against the upper panes of glass; two calves were bawling from the barnyard, where some of the men were at work loading a dump-cart and shouting as if every one were deaf. There was a cheerful feeling of activity, and even an air of comfort, about the Byfleet Poor-house. Almost every one was possessed of a most interesting past, though there was less to be said about the future. The inmates were by no means distressed or unhappy; many of them retired to this shelter only for the winter season, and would go out presently, some to begin such work as they could still do, others to live in their own small houses; old age had impoverished most of them by limiting their power of endurance; but far from lamenting the fact that they were town charges, they rather liked the change and excitement of a winter residence on the poor-farm. There was a sharp-faced, hard-worked young widow with seven children, who was an exception to the general level of society, because she deplored the change in her fortunes. The older women regarded her with suspicion, and were apt to talk about her in moments like this, when they happened to sit together at their work.

The three bean-pickers were dressed alike in stout brown ginghams, checked by a white line, and all wore great faded aprons of blue drilling, with sufficient pockets convenient to the right hand. Miss Peggy Bond was a very small, belligerent-looking person, who wore a huge pair of steel-bowed spectacles, holding her sharp chin well up in air, as if to supplement an inadequate nose. She was more than half blind, but the spectacles seemed to face upward instead of square ahead, as if their wearer were always on the sharp lookout for birds. Miss Bond had suffered much personal damage from time to time, because she never took heed where she planted her feet, and so was always tripping and stubbing her bruised way through the world. She had fallen down hatchways and cellarways, and stepped composedly into deep ditches and pasture brooks; but she was proud of stating that she was upsighted, and so was her father before her. At the poorhouse, where an unusual malady was considered a distinction, upsightedness was looked upon as a most honorable infirmity. Plain rheumatism, such as afflicted Aunt Lavina Dow, whose twisted hands found even this light work difficult and tiresome, — plain rheumatism was something of every-day occurrence, and nobody cared to hear about it. Poor Peggy was a meek and friendly soul, who never put herself forward; she was just like other folks, as she always loved to say, but Mrs. Lavina Dow was a different sort of person altogether, of great dignity and, occasionally, almost aggressive behavior. The time had been when she could do a good day's work with anybody: but for many years now she had not left the town-farm, being too badly crippled to work; she had no relations or friends to visit, but from an innate love of authority she could not submit to being one of those who are forgotten by the world. Mrs. Dow was the hostess and social lawgiver here, where she remembered every inmate and every item of interest for nearly forty years, besides an immense amount of town history and biography for three or four generations back.

She was the dear friend of the third woman, Betsey Lane; together they led thought and opinion — chiefly opinion — and held sway, not only over Byfleet Poor-farm, but also the selectmen and all others in authority. Betsey Lane had spent most of her life as aid-in-general to the respected household of old General Thornton. She had been much trusted and valued, and, at the breaking up of that once large and flourishing family, she had been left in good circumstances, what with legacies and her own comfortable savings; but by sad misfortune and lavish generosity everything had been scattered, and after much illness, which ended in a stiffened arm and more uncertainty, the good soul had sensibly decided that it was easier for the whole town to support her than for a part of it. She had always hoped to see something of the world before she died; she came of an adventurous, seafaring stock, but had never made a longer journey than to the towns of Danby and Northville, thirty miles away.

They were all old women; but Betsey Lane, who was sixty-nine, and looked much older, was the youngest. Peggy Bond was far on in the seventies, and Mrs. Dow was at least ten years older. She made a great secret of her years; and as she sometimes spoke of events prior to the Revolution with the assertion of having been an eye-witness, she naturally wore an air of vast antiquity. Her tales were an inexpressible delight to Betsey Lane, who felt younger by twenty years because her friend and comrade was so unconscious of chronological limitations.

The bushel basket of cranberry beans was within easy reach, and each of the pickers had filled her lap from it again and again. The shed chamber was not an unpleasant place in which to sit at work, with its traces of seed corn hanging from the brown cross-beams, its spare churns, and dusty loom, and rickety wool-wheels, and a few bits of old furniture. In one far corner was a wide board of dismal use and suggestion, and close beside it an old cradle. There was a battered chest of drawers where the keeper of the poor-house kept his garden-seeds, with the withered remains of three seed cucumbers ornamenting the top. Nothing beautiful could be discovered, nothing interesting, but there was something usable and homely about the place. It was the favorite and untroubled bower of the bean-pickers, to which they might retreat unmolested from the public apartments of this rustic institution.

. Betsey Lane blew away the chaff from her handful of beans. The spring breeze blew the chaff back again, and sifted it over her face and shoulders. She rubbed it out of her eyes impatiently, and happened to notice old Peggy holding her own handful high, as if it were an oblation, and turning her queer, up-tilted head this way and that, to look at the beans sharply, as if she were first cousin to a hen.

"There, Miss Bond, 't is kind of botherin' work for you, ain't it?" Betsey inquired compassionately.

"I feel to enjoy it, anything that I can do my own way so," responded Peggy. "I like to do my part. Ain't that old Mis' Fales comin' up the road? It sounds like her step."

The others looked, but they were not far-sighted, and for a moment Peggy had the advantage. Mrs. Fales was not a favorite.

"I hope she ain't comin' here to put up this spring. I guess she won't now, it 's gettin' so late," said Betsey Lane. "She likes to go rovin' soon as the roads is settled."

"'T is Mis' Fales!" said Peggy Bond, listening with solemn anxiety. "There, do let 's pray her by!"

"I guess she 's headin' for her cousin's folks up Beech Hill way," said Betsey presently. "If she 'd left her daughter's this mornin', she 'd have got just about as far as this. I kind o' wish she had stepped in just to pass the time o' day, long 's she wa'n't going to make no stop."

There was a silence as to further speech in the shed chamber; and even the calves were quiet in the barnyard. The men had all gone away to the field where corn-planting was going on. The beans clicked steadily into the wooden measure at the pickers' feet.

Betsey Lane began to sing a hymn, and the others joined in as best they might, like autumnal crickets; their voices were sharp and cracked, with now and then a few low notes of plaintive tone. Betsey herself could sing pretty well, but the others could only make a kind of accompaniment. Their voices ceased altogether at the higher notes.

"Oh my! I wish I had the means to go to the Centennial," mourned Betsey Lane, stopping so suddenly that the others had to go on croaking and shrilling without her for a moment before they could stop. "It seems to me as if I can't die happy 'less I do," she added; "I ain't never seen nothin' of the world, an' here I be."

"What if you was as old as I be?" suggested Mrs. Dow pompously. "You've got time enough yet, Betsey; don't you go an' despair. I knowed of a woman that went clean round the world four times when she was past eighty, an' enjoyed herself real well. Her folks followed the sea; she had three sons an' a daughter married, — all shipmasters, and she'd been with her own husband when they was young. She was left a widder early, and fetched up her family herself, — a real stirrin', smart woman. After they 'd got married off, an' settled, an' was doing well, she come to be lonesome; and first she tried to stick it out alone, but she wa'n't one that could; an' she got a notion she had n't nothin' before her but her last sickness, and she wa'n't a person that enjoyed havin' other folks do for her. So one on her boys — I guess 't was the oldest — said he was going to take her to sea; there was ample room, an' he was sailin' a good time o' year for the Cape o' Good Hope an' way up to some o' them tea-ports in the Chiny Seas. She was all high to go, but it made a sight o' talk at her age; an' the minister made it a subject o' prayer the last Sunday, and all the folks took a last leave; but she said to some she 'd fetch 'em home something real pritty, and so did. An' then they come home t' other way, round the Horn, an' she done so well, an' was such a sight o' company, the other child'n was jealous, an' she promised she 'd go a v'y'ge long o' each on 'em. She was as sprightly a person as ever I see; an' could speak well o' what she 'd seen."

"Did she die to sea?" asked Peggy, with interest.

"No, she died to home between v'y'ges,

or she 'd gone to sea again. I was to her funeral. She liked her son George's ship the best; 't was the one she was going on to Callao. They said the men aboard all called her 'gran'ma'am,' an' she kep' 'em mended up, an' would go below and tend to 'em if they was sick. She might 'a' been alive an' enjoyin' of herself a good many years but for the kick of a cow; 't was a new cow out of a drove, a dreadful unruly beast."

Mrs. Dow stopped for breath, and reached down for a new supply of beans; her empty apron was gray with soft chaff. Betsey Lane, still pondering on the Centennial, began to sing another verse of her hymn, and again the old women joined her. At this moment some strangers came driving round into the yard from the front of the house. The turf was soft, and our friends did not hear the horses' steps. Their voices cracked and quavered; it was a funny little concert, and a lady in an open carriage just below listened with sympathy and amusement.

II.

"Betsey! Betsey! Miss Lane!" a voice called eagerly at the foot of the stairs that led up from the shed. "Betsey! There's a lady here wants to see you right away."

Betsey was dazed with excitement, like a country child who knows the rare pleasure of being called out of school. "Lor', I ain't fit to go down, be I?" she faltered, looking anxiously at her friends; but Peggy was gazing even nearer to the zenith than usual, in her excited effort to see down into the yard, and Mrs. Dow only nodded somewhat jealously, and said that she guessed 't was nobody would do her any harm. She rose ponderously, while Betsey hesitated, being, as they would have said, all of a twitter. "It is a lady, certain," Mrs. Dow assured her; "'t ain't often there's a lady comes here."

"While there was any of Mis' Gen'ral Thornton's folks left, I wa'n't without visits from the gentry," said Betsey Lane, turning back proudly at the head of the stairs, with a touch of old-world pride and sense of high station. Then she disappeared, and closed the door behind her at the stair-foot with a decision quite unwelcome to the friends above.

"She need n't 'a' been so dreadful 'fraid anybody was goin' to listen. I guess we've got folks to ride an' see us, or had once, if we hain't now," said Miss Peggy Bond, plaintively.

" I expect 't was only the wind shoved it to," said Aunt Lavina. "Betsey is one that gits flustered easier than some. I wish 't was somebody to take her off an' give her a kind of a good time ; she 's young to settle down 'long of old folks like us. Betsey 's got a notion o' rovin' such as ain't my na- tur', but I should like to see her satisfied. She 'd been a very understandin' person, if she had the advantages that some does."

" 'T is so," said Peggy Bond, tilting her chin high. " I suppose you can't hear nothin' they 're saying ? I feel my hearin' ain't up to whar it was. I can hear things close to me well as ever ; but there, hearin' ain't everything ; 't ain't as if we lived where there was more goin' on to hear. Seems to me them folks is stoppin' a good while."

" They surely be," agreed Lavina Dow.

" I expect it 's somethin' particular. There ain't none of the Thornton folks left, except one o' the gran'darters, an' I 've often heard Betsey remark that she should never see her more, for she lives to London. Strange how folks feels contented in them strayaway places off to the ends of the airth."

The flies and bees were buzzing against the hot window-panes ; the handfuls of beans were clicking into the brown wooden measure. A bird came and perched on the window-sill, and then flitted away toward the blue sky. Below, in the yard, Betsey Lane stood talking with the lady. She had put her blue drilling apron over her head, and her face was shining with delight.

"Lor', dear," she said, for at least the third time, " I remember ye when I first see ye; an awful pritty baby you was, an' they all said you looked just like the old gen'ral. Be you goin' back to foreign parts right away?"

"Yes, I'm going back; you know that all my children are there. I wish I could take you with me for a visit," said the charming young guest. "I'm going to carry over some of the pictures and furniture from the old house; I didn't care half so much for them when I was younger as I do now. Perhaps next summer we shall all come over for a while. I should like to see my girls and boys playing under the pines."

"I wish you re'lly was livin' to the old

place," said Betsey Lane. Her imagination was not swift; she needed time to think over all that was being told her, and she could not fancy the two strange houses across the sea. The old Thornton house was to her mind the most delightful and elegant in the world.

"Is there anything I can do for you?" asked Mrs. Strafford kindly, — "anything that I can do for you myself, before I go away? I shall be writing to you, and sending some pictures of the children, and you must let me know how you are getting on."

"Yes, there is one thing, darlin'. If you could stop in the village an' pick me out a pritty, little, small lookin'-glass, that I can keep for my own an' have to remember you by. 'T ain't that I want to set me above the rest o' the folks, but I was always used to havin' my own when I was to your grandma's. There 's very nice folks here, some on 'em, and I 'm better off than if I was able to keep house ; but sence you ask me, that 's the only thing I feel cropin' about. What be you goin' right back for ? ain't you goin' to see the great fair to Pheladelphy, that everybody talks about?"

"No," said Mrs. Strafford, laughing at

this eager and almost convicting question. "No; I'm going back next week. If I were, I believe that I should take you with me. Good-by, dear old Betsey; you make me feel as if I were a little girl again; you look just the same."

For full five minutes the old woman stood out in the sunshine, dazed with delight, and majestic with a sense of her own consequence. She held something tight in her hand, without thinking what it might be; but just as the friendly mistress of the poor-farm came out to hear the news, she tucked the roll of money into the bosom of her brown gingham dress. "'T was my dear Mis' Katy Strafford," she turned to say proudly. "She come way over from London; she's been sick; they thought the voyage would do her good. She said most the first thing she had on her mind was to come an' find me, and see how I was, an' if I was comfortable; an' now she's goin' right back. She's got two splendid houses; an' said how she wished I was there to look after things, — she remembered I was always her gran'ma's right hand. Oh, it does so carry me back, to see her! Seems if all the rest on 'em must be there together to the old house. There, I must go right up an' tell Mis' Dow an' Peggy."

"Dinner's all ready; I was just goin' to blow the horn for the men-folks," said the keeper's wife. "They'll be right down. I expect you've got along smart with them beans, — all three of you together;" but Betsey's mind roved so high and so far at that moment that no achievements of bean-picking could lure it back.

III.

The long table in the great kitchen soon gathered its company of waifs and strays, — creatures of improvidence and misfortune, and the irreparable victims of old age. The dinner was satisfactory, and there was not much delay for conversation. Peggy Bond and Mrs. Dow and Betsey Lane always sat together at one end, with an air of putting the rest of the company below the salt. Betsey was still flushed with excitement; in fact, she could not eat as much as usual, and she looked up from time to time expectantly, as if she were likely to be asked to speak of her guest; but everybody was hungry, and even Mrs. Dow broke in upon some attempted confidences by asking inopportunely for a second potato. There were nearly twenty at the table, counting the keeper and his wife and two children, noisy little persons who had come from school with the small flock belonging to the poor widow, who sat just opposite our friends. She finished her dinner before any one else, and pushed her chair back; she always helped with the housework, — a thin, sorry, bad-tempered-looking poor soul, whom grief had sharpened instead of softening. " I expect you feel too fine to set with common folks," she said enviously to Betsey.

" Here I be a-settin'," responded Betsey calmly. " I don' know 's I behave more unbecomin' than usual." Betsey prided herself upon her good and proper manners; but the rest of the company, who would have liked to hear the bit of morning news, were now defrauded of that pleasure. The wrong note had been struck; there was a silence after the clatter of knives and plates, and one by one the cheerful town charges disappeared. The bean-picking had been finished, and there was a call for any of the women who felt like planting corn; so Peggy Bond, who could follow the line of hills pretty fairly, and Betsey herself, who was still equal to anybody at that work, and Mrs. Dow, all went out to the field together. Aunt La-vina labored slowly up the yard, carrying a light splint-bottomed kitchen chair and her knitting-work, and sat near the stone wall on a gentle rise, where she could see the pond and the green country, and exchange a word with her friends as they came and went up and down the rows. Betsey vouchsafed a word now and then about Mrs. Strafford, but you would have thought that she had been suddenly elevated to Mrs. Strafford's own cares and the responsibilities attending them, and had little in common with her old as-sociates. Mrs. Dow and Peggy knew well that these high-feeling times never lasted long, and so they waited with as much pa-tience as they could muster. They were by no means without that true tact which is only another word for unselfish sympathy.

The strip of corn land ran along the side of a great field; at the upper end of it was a field-corner thicket of young maples and walnut saplings, the children of a great nut-tree that marked the boundary. Once, when Betsey Lane found herself alone near this

shelter at the end of her row, the other plant-
ers having lagged behind beyond the rising
ground, she looked stealthily about, and then
put her hand inside her gown, and for the
first time took out the money that Mrs.
Strafford had given her. She turned it over
and over with an astonished look: there
were new bank-bills for a hundred dollars.
Betsey gave a funny little shrug of her
shoulders, came out of the bushes, and took
a step or two on the narrow edge of turf,
as if she were going to dance; then she hastily tucked away her treasure, and stepped
discreetly down into the soft harrowed and
hoed land, and began to drop corn again,
five kernels to a hill. She had seen the top
of Peggy Bond's head over the knoll, and
now Peggy herself came entirely into view,
gazing upward to the skies, and stumbling
more or less, but counting the corn by touch
and twisting her head about anxiously to
gain advantage over her uncertain vision.
Betsey made a friendly, inarticulate little
sound as they passed; she was thinking that
somebody said once that Peggy's eyesight
might be remedied if she could go to Boston
to the hospital; but that was so remote and
impossible an undertaking that no one had

ever taken the first step. Betsey Lane's brown old face suddenly worked with excitement, but in a moment more she regained her usual firm expression, and spoke carelessly to Peggy as she turned and came alongside.

The high spring wind of the morning had quite fallen; it was a lovely May afternoon. The woods about the field to the northward were full of birds, and the young leaves scarcely hid the solemn shapes of a company of crows that patiently attended the corn-planting. Two of the men had finished their hoeing, and were busy with the construction of a scarecrow; they knelt in the furrows, chuckling, and looking over some forlorn, discarded garments. It was a time-honored custom to make the scarecrow resemble one of the poor-house family; and this year they intended to have Mrs. Lavina Dow protect the field in effigy; last year it was the counterfeit of Betsey Lane who stood on guard, with an easily recognized quilted hood and the remains of a valued shawl that one of the calves had found airing on a fence and chewed to pieces. Behind the men was the foundation for this rustic attempt at statuary, — an upright stake and bar in the form of a cross. This stood on the highest part of the field; and as the men knelt near it, and the quaint figures of the corn-planters went and came, the scene gave a curious suggestion of foreign life. It was not like New England; the presence of the rude cross appealed strangely to the imagination.

IV.

Life flowed so smoothly, for the most part, at the Byfleet Poor-farm, that nobody knew what to make, later in the summer, of a strange disappearance. All the elder inmates were familiar with illness and death, and the poor pomp of a town-pauper's funeral. The comings and goings and the various misfortunes of those who composed this strange family, related only through its disasters, hardly served for the excitement and talk of a single day. Now that the June days were at their longest, the old people were sure to wake earlier than ever; but one morning, to the astonishment of every one, Betsey Lane's bed was empty; the sheets and blankets, which were her own, and guarded with jealous care, were carefully folded and placed on a chair not too near the window, and Betsey had flown. Nobody had heard her go down the creaking stairs. The kitchen door was unlocked, and the old watch-dog lay on the step outside in the early sunshine, wagging his tail and looking wise, as if he were left on guard and meant to keep the fugitive's secret.

"Never knowed her to do nothin' afore 'thout talking it over a fortnight, and paradin' off when we could all see her," ventured a spiteful voice. "Guess we can wait till night to hear 'bout it."

Mrs. Dow looked sorrowful and shook her head. "Betsey had an aunt on her mother's side that went and drownded of herself; she was a pritty-appearing woman as ever you see."

"Perhaps she's gone to spend the· day with Decker's folks," suggested Peggy Bond. "She always takes an extra early start; she was speakin' lately o' going up their way;" but Mrs. Dow shook her head with a most melancholy look. "I'm impressed that something's befell her," she insisted. "I heard her a-groanin' in her sleep. I was wakeful the forepart o' the night, — 't is very unusual with me, too."

" 'T wa'n't like Betsey not to leave us any word," said the other old friend, with more resentment than melancholy. They sat together almost in silence that morning in the shed chamber. Mrs. Dow was sorting and cutting rags, and Peggy braided them into long ropes, to be made into mats at a later date. If they had only known where Betsey Lane had gone, they might have talked about it until dinner - time at noon; but failing this new subject, they could take no interest in any of their old ones. Out in the field the corn was well up, and the men were hoeing. It was a hot morning in the shed chamber, and the woolen rags were dusty and hot to handle.

V.

Byfleet people knew each other well, and when this mysteriously absent person did not return to the town-farm at the end of a week, public interest became much excited ; and presently it was ascertained that Betsey Lane was neither making a visit to her friends the Deckers on Birch Hill, nor to any nearer acquaintances ; in fact, she had disappeared altogether from her wonted haunts. Nobody remembered to have seen her pass, hers had been such an early flitting; and when somebody thought of her having gone away by train, he was laughed at for forgetting that the earliest morning train from South Byfleet, the nearest station, did not start until long after eight o'clock; and if Betsey had designed to be one of the passengers, she would have started along the road at seven, and been seen and known of all women. There was not a kitchen in that part of Byfleet that did not have windows toward the road. Conversation rarely left the level of the neighborhood gossip: to see Betsey Lane, in her best clothes, at that hour in the morning, would have been the signal for much exercise of imagination; but as day after day went by without news, the curiosity of those who knew her best turned slowly into fear, and at last Peggy Bond again gave utterance to the belief that Betsey had either gone out in the early morning and put an end to her life, or that she had gone to the Centennial. Some of the people at table were moved to loud laughter, — it was at supper-time on a Sunday night, — but others listened with great interest.

" She never 'd put on her good clothes to drownd herself," said the widow. " She might have thought 't was good as takin' 'em with her, though. Old folks has wandered off an' got lost in the woods afore now."

Mrs. Dow and Peggy resented this impertinent remark, but deigned to take no notice of the speaker. " She would n't have wore her best clothes to the Centennial, would she ?" mildly inquired Peggy, bobbing her head toward the ceiling. " 'T would be a shame to spoil your best things in such a place. An' I don't know of her havin' any money; there 's the end o' that."

" You 're bad as old Mis' Bland, that used to live neighbor to our folks," said one of the old men. " She was dreadful precise ; an' she so begretched to wear a good alapaca dress that was left to her, that it hung in a press forty year, an' baited the moths at last."

" I often seen Mis' Bland a-goin' in to meetin' when I was a young girl," said Peggy Bond approvingly. " She was a good-appearin' woman, an' she left property."

" Wish she 'd left it to me, then," said the poor soul opposite, glancing at her pathetic row of children : but it was not good manners at the farm to deplore one's situation, and Mrs. Dow and Peggy only frowned. "Where do you suppose Betsey can be?" said Mrs. Dow, for the twentieth time. "She did n't have no money. I know she ain't gone far, if it 's so that she 's yet alive. She 's b'en real pinched all the spring."

"Perhaps that lady that come one day give her some," the keeper's wife suggested mildly.

"Then Betsey would have told me," said Mrs. Dow, with injured dignity.

VI.

On the morning of her disappearance, Betsey rose even before the pewee and the English sparrow, and dressed herself quietly, though with trembling hands, and stole out of the kitchen door like a plunderless thief. The old dog licked her hand and looked at her anxiously; the tortoise-shell cat rubbed against her best gown, and trotted away up the yard, then she turned anxiously and came after the old woman, following faithfully until she had to be driven back. Betsey was used to long country excursions afoot. She dearly loved the early morning; and finding that there was no dew to trouble her, she began to follow pasture paths and short cuts across the fields, surprising here and there a flock of sleepy sheep, or a startled calf that rustled out from the bushes. The birds were pecking their breakfast from bush and turf; and hardly any of the wild inhabitants of that rural world were enough alarmed by her presence to do more than flutter away if they chanced to be in her path. She stepped along, light-footed and eager as a girl, dressed in her neat old straw bonnet and black gown, and carrying a few belongings in her best bundle-handkerchief, one that her only brother had brought home from the East Indies fifty years before. There was an old crow perched as sentinel on a small, dead pine-tree, where he could warn friends who were pulling up the sprouted corn in a field close by; but he only gave a contemptuous caw as the adventurer appeared, and she shook her bundle at him in revenge, and laughed to see him so clumsy as he tried to keep his footing on the twigs.

"Yes, I be," she assured him. "I'm a-goin' to Pheladelphy, to the Centennial, same 's other folks. I 'd jest as soon tell ye 's not, old crow; " and Betsey laughed aloud in pleased content with herself and her daring, as she walked along. She had only two miles to go to the station at South Byfleet, and she felt for the money now and then, and found it safe enough. She took great pride in the success of her escape, and especially in the long concealment of her wealth. Not a night had passed since Mrs. Strafford's visit that she had not slept with the roll of money under her pillow by night, and buttoned safe inside her dress by day. She knew that everybody would offer advice and even commands about the spending or saving of it; and she brooked no interference.

The last mile of the foot-path to South Byfleet was along the railway track; and Betsey began to feel in haste, though it was still nearly two hours to train time. She looked anxiously forward and back along the rails every few minutes, for fear of being run over; and at last she caught sight of an engine that was apparently coming toward her, and took flight into the woods before she could gather courage to follow the path again. The freight train proved to be at a standstill, waiting at a turnout; and some of the men were straying about, eating their early breakfast comfortably in this time of leisure. As the old woman came up to them, she stopped too, for a moment of rest and conversation.

"Where be ye goin'?" she asked pleasantly; and they told her. It was to the town where she had to change cars and take the great through train ; a point of geography which she had learned from evening talks between the men at the farm.

"What 'll ye carry me there for?"

"We don't run no passenger cars," said one of the young fellows, laughing. "What makes you in such a hurry?"

"I 'm startin' for Pheladelphy, an' it 's a gre't ways to go."

"So 't is ; but you 're consid'able early, if you 're makin' for the eight-forty train. See here! you have n't got a needle an' thread 'long of you in that bundle, have you? If you 'll sew me on a couple o' buttons, I 'll give ye a free ride. I 'm in a sight o' distress, an' none o' the fellows is provided with as much as a bent pin."

"You poor boy! I 'll have you seen to, in half a minute. I 'm troubled with a stiff arm, but I 'll do the best I can."

The obliging Betsey seated herself stiffly on the slope of the embankment, and found her thread and needle with utmost haste. Two of the train-men stood by and watched the careful stitches, and even offered her a place as spare brakeman, so that they might keep her near; and Betsey took the offer with considerable seriousness, only thinking it necessary to assure them that she was getting most too old to be out in all weathers. An express went by like an earthquake, and she was presently hoisted on board an empty box-car by two of her new and flattering acquaintances, and found herself before noon at the end of the first stage of her journey, without having spent a cent, and furnished with any amount of thrifty advice. One of the young men, being compassionate of her unprotected state as a traveler, advised her to find out the widow of an uncle of his in Philadelphia, saying despairingly that he could n't tell her just how to find the house; but Miss Betsey Lane said that she had an English tongue in her head, and should be sure to find whatever she was looking for. This unexpected incident of the freight train was the reason why everybody about the

South Byfleet station insisted that no such person had taken passage by the regular train that same morning, and why there were those who persuaded themselves that Miss Betsey Lane was probably lying at the bottom of the poor-farm pond.

VII.

"Land sakes!" said Miss Betsey Lane, as she watched a Turkish person parading by in his red fez, "I call the Centennial somethin' like the day o' judgment! I wish I was goin' to stop a month, but I dare say 't would be the death o' my poor old bones."

She was leaning against the barrier of a patent pop-corn establishment, which had given her a sudden reminder of home, and of the winter nights when the sharp-kerneled little red and yellow ears were brought out, and Old Uncle Eph Flanders sat by the kitchen stove, and solemnly filled a great wooden chopping-tray for the refreshment of the company. She had wandered and loitered and looked until her eyes and head had grown numb and unreceptive; but it is only unimaginative persons who can be really astonished.   The imagination can always outrun the possible and actual sights and sounds of the world ; and this plain old body from Byfleet rarely found anything rich and splendid enough to surprise her. She saw the wonders of the West and the splendors of the East with equal calmness and satisfaction ; she had always known that there was an amazing world outside the boundaries of Byfleet.   There was a piece of paper in her pocket on which was marked, in her clumsy handwriting, " If Betsey Lane should meet with accident, notify the selectmen of Byfleet; " but having made this slight provision for the future, she had thrown herself boldly into the sea of strangers, and then had made the joyful discovery that friends were to be found at every turn.

There was something delightfully companionable about Betsey ; she had a way of suddenly looking up over her big spectacles with a reassuring and expectant smile, as if you were going to speak to her, and you generally did.   She must have found out where hundreds of people came from, and whom they had left at home, and what they thought of the great show, as she sat on a bench to rest, or leaned over the railings where free luncheons were afforded by the makers of hot waffles and molasses candy and fried potatoes; and there was not a night when she did not return to her lodgings with a pocket crammed with samples of spool cotton and nobody knows what. She had already collected small presents for almost everybody she knew at home, and she was such a pleasant, beaming old country body, so unmistakably appreciative and interested, that nobody ever thought of wishing that she would move on. Nearly all the busy people of the Exhibition called her either Aunty or Grandma at once, and made little pleasures for her as best they could. She was a delightful contrast to the indifferent, stupid crowd that drifted along, with eyes fixed at the same level, and seeing, even on that level, nothing for fifty feet at a time. "What be you making here, dear?" Betsey Lane would ask joyfully, and the most perfunctory guardian hastened to explain. She squandered money as she had never had the pleasure of doing before, and this hastened the day when she must return to Byfleet. She was always inquiring if there were any spectacle-sellers at hand, and received occasional directions ; but it was a difficult place for her to find her way about in, and the very last day of her stay arrived before she found an exhibitor of the desired sort, an oculist and instrument-maker.

"I called to get some specs for a friend that 's upsighted," she gravely informed the salesman, to his extreme amusement. "She 's dreadful troubled, and jerks her head up like a hen a-drinkin'. She 's got a blur a-growin' an' spreadin', an' sometimes she can see out to one side on 't, and more times she can't."

"Cataracts," said a middle-aged gentleman at her side ; and Betsey Lane turned to regard him with approval and curiosity.

"'T is Miss Peggy Bond I was mentioning, of Byfleet Poor-farm," she explained. "I count on gettin' some glasses to relieve her trouble, if there 's any to be found."

"Glasses won't do her any good," said the stranger. "Suppose you come and sit down on this bench, and tell me all about it. First, where is Byfleet ?" and Betsey gave the directions at length.

"I thought so," said the surgeon. "How old is this friend of yours ?"

Betsey cleared her throat decisively, and

smoothed her gown over her knees as if it were an apron; then she turned to take a good look at her new acquaintance as they sat on the rustic bench together. " Who be you, sir, I should like to know ? " she asked, in a friendly tone.

" My name 's Dunster."

" I take it you 're a doctor," continued Betsey, as if they had overtaken each other walking from Byfleet to South Byfleet on a summer morning.

" I 'm a doctor; part of one at least," said he. " I know more or less about eyes ; and I spend my summers down on the shore at the mouth of your river; some day I 'll come up and look at this person. How old is she ? "

" Peggy Bond is one that never tells her age; 't ain't come quite up to where she 'll begin to brag of it, you see," explained Betsey reluctantly; " but I know her to be nigh to seventy-six, one way or t' other. Her an' Mrs. Mary Ann Chick was same year's child'n, and Peggy knows I know it, an' two or three times when we 've be'n in the buryin'-ground where Mary Ann lays an' has her dates right on her headstone, I could n't bring Peggy to take no sort o' notice. I will say she makes, at times, a convenience of being upsighted. But there, I feel for her, — everybody does; it keeps her stubbin' an' trippin' against everything, beakin' and gazin' up the way she has to."

"Yes, yes," said the doctor, whose eyes were twinkling. "I 'll come and look after her, with your town doctor, this summer, — some time in the last of July or first of August."

"You 'll find occupation," said Betsey, not without an air of patronage. "Most of us to the Byfleet Farm has got our ails, now I tell ye. You ain't got no bitters that 'll take a dozen years right off an ol' lady's shoulders ?"

The busy man smiled pleasantly, and shook his head as he went away. "Dunster," said Betsey to herself, soberly committing the new name to her sound memory. "Yes, I must n't forget to speak of him to the doctor, as he directed. I do' know now as Peggy would vally herself quite so much accordin' to, if she had her eyes fixed same as other folks. I expect there would n't been a smarter woman in town, though, if she 'd had a proper chance. Now I 've done what I set to do for her, I do believe, an' 't wa'n't glasses, neither. I 'll git her a pritty little shawl with that money I laid aside. Peggy Bond ain't got a pritty shawl. I always wanted to have a real good time, an' now I 'm havin' it."

VIII.

Two or three days later, two pathetic figures might have been seen crossing the slopes of the poor-farm field, toward the low shores of Byfield pond. It was early in the morning, and the stubble of the lately mown grass was wet with rain and hindering to old feet. Peggy Bond was more blundering and liable to stray in the wrong direction than usual; it was one of the days when she could hardly see at all. Aunt Lavina Dow was unusually clumsy of movement, and stiff in the joints; she had not been so far from the house for three years. The morning breeze filled the gathers of her wide gingham skirt, and aggravated the size of her unwieldy figure. She supported herself with a stick, and trusted beside to the fragile support of Peggy's arm. They were talking together in whispers.

"Oh, my sakes!" exclaimed Peggy, moving her small head from side to side. "Hear you wheeze, Mis' Dow! This may be the death o' you; there, do go slow! You set here on the side-hill, an' le' me go try if I can see."

"It needs more eyesight than you 've got," said Mrs. Dow, panting between the words. "Oh! to think how spry I was in my young days, an' here I be now, the full of a door, an' all my complaints so aggravated by my size. 'T is hard! 't is hard! but I 'm a-doin' of all this for pore Betsey's sake. I know they 've all laughed, but I look to see her ris' to the top o' the pond this day, — 't is just nine days since she departed; an' say what they may, I know she hove herself in. It run in her family; Betsey had an aunt that done just so, an' she ain't be'n like herself, a-broodin' an' hivin' away alone, an' nothin' to say to you an' me that was always sich good company all together. Somethin' sprung her mind, now I tell ye, Mis' Bond."

"I feel to hope we sha'n't find her, I must say," faltered Peggy. It was plain that Mrs. Dow was the captain of this doleful expedition. "I guess she ain't never

thought o' drowndin' of herself, Mis' Dow;
she 's gone off a-visitin' way over to the
other side o' South Byfleet; some thinks
she 's gone to the Centennial even now!"

"She had n't no proper means, I tell ye,"
wheezed Mrs. Dow indignantly; "an' if
you prefer that others should find her
floatin' to the top this day, instid of us
that 's her best friends, you can step back
to the house."

They walked on in aggrieved silence.
Peggy Bond trembled with excitement, but
her companion's firm grasp never wavered,
and so they came to the narrow, gravelly
margin and stood still. Peggy tried in vain
to see the glittering water and the pond-
lilies that starred it; she knew that they
must be there; once, years ago, she had
caught fleeting glimpses of them, and she
never forgot what she had once seen. The
clear blue sky overhead, the dark pine-woods
beyond the pond, were all clearly pictured in
her mind. "Can't you see nothin'?" she
faltered; "I believe I 'm wuss 'n upsighted
this day. I 'm going to be blind."

"No," said Lavina Dow solemnly; "no,
there ain't nothin' whatever, Peggy. I hope
to mercy she ain't" —

"Why, whoever 'd expected to find you 'way out here·!" exclaimed a brisk and cheerful voice. There stood Betsey Lane herself, close behind them, having just emerged from a thicket of alders that grew close by. She was following the short way homeward from the railroad.

"Why, what 's the matter, Mis' Dow? You ain't overdoin', be ye? an' Peggy 's all of a flutter. What in the name o' natur' ails ye?"

"There ain't nothin' the matter, as I knows on," responded the leader of this fruitless expedition. "We only thought we 'd take a stroll this pleasant mornin'," she added, with sublime self-possession. "Where 've you be'n, Betsey Lane?"

"To Pheladelphy, ma'am," said Betsey, looking quite young and gay, and wearing a townish and unfamiliar air that upheld her words. "All ought to go that can; why, you feel 's if you 'd be'n all round the world. I guess I 've got enough to think of and tell ye for the rest o' my days. I 've always wanted to go somewheres. I wish you 'd be'n there, I do so. I 've talked with folks from Chiny an' the back o' Pennsylvany: and I see folks way from Australy that 'peared as well as anybody; an' I see how they made spool cotton, an' sights o' other things; an' I spoke with a doctor that lives down to the beach in the summer, an' he offered to come up 'long in the first of August, an' see what he can do for Peggy's eyesight. There was di'monds there as big as pigeon's eggs; an' I met with Mis' Abby Fletcher from South Byfleet depot; an' there was hogs there that weighed risin' thirteen hunderd " —

" I want to know," said Mrs. Lavina Dow and Peggy Bond, together.

" Well, 't was a great exper'ence for a person," added Lavina, turning ponderously, in spite of herself, to give a last wistful look at the smiling waters of the pond.

" I don't know how soon I be goin' to settle down," proclaimed the rustic sister of Sindbad. " What 's for the good o' one 's for the good of all. You just wait till we 're setting together up in the old shed chamber! You know, my dear Mis' Katy Strafford give me a han'some present o' money that day she come to see me; and I 'd be'n a-dreamin' by night an' day o' seein' that Centennial; and when I come to think on 't I felt sure somebody ought to go from this neighborhood, if 't was only for the good o' the rest; and I thought I'd better be the one. I wa'n't goin' to ask the selec'men neither. I 've come back with one-thirty-five in money, and I see everything there, an' I fetched ye all a little somethin'; but I 'm full o' dust now, an' pretty nigh beat out. I never see a place more friendly than Pheladelphy; but 't ain't natural to a Byfleet person to be always walkin' on a level. There, now, Peggy, you take my bundle-handkercher and the basket, and let Mis' Dow sag on to me. I 'll git her along twice as easy."

With this the small elderly company set forth triumphant toward the poor-house, across the wide green field.

BETWEEN MASS AND VESPERS.

MASS was over; the noonday sun was so bright at the church door that, instead of waiting there in a sober expectant group, three middle-aged men of the parish went a few steps westward to stand in the shade of a great maple-tree. There they stood watching the people go by — the small boys and the chattering girls. Now and then one of the older men or women said a few words in Irish to Dennis Call or John Mulligan by way of friendly salutation. They were a contented, pleasant-looking flock, these parishioners of St. Anne's; they might have lost the gayety that they would have kept in the old country, but a look of good cheer had not forsaken them, though many a figure showed the thinness that comes from steady, hard work, and almost every face had the deep lines that are worn only by anxiety. The pretty girls looked as their mothers had looked before them, only they were not so fair and fresh-colored, having been brought up less wholesomely and too much indoors.

"That's a nice gerrl o' Mary Finnerty's," said Dennis Call, gravely, to his mates, following the charming young creature with approving eyes.

"'Deed, then, you're right, Dinny," agreed little Pat Finn, a queer old figure of a shoemaker, who was bent nearly double between the effects of his stooping trade and a natural warp in his bones. "There don't be so pritty a little gerrl as Katy Finnerty walk into church, so there don't! I like her meself; she's got the cut o' the gerrls in Tralee — the prittiest gerrls is in it that's in the whole of Ireland."

"Coom now, then! you do always be bragging for Tralee; there's enough other places as good as it," scoffed Dennis. "Anybody that ain't a Bantry man can tark as they like, they'll have to put up wid second-best whin all's said an' done."

"Whisht now!" said John Mulligan, putting his hand to his forehead and bobbing his head respectfully at Father Ryan, the old priest, who had just come hurrying from the vestry door along a precarious footway of single boards left there since the days of spring mud.

"I hope you 're feeling fine the day, sir?" said little Pat Finn, looking up with friendliness and pride at the tall old man. "We 're getting good weather now, thank God, sir."

"We are that, Patrick Finn. God bless you, boys!" And Father Ryan went past them down the street to his house, while they all watched him without speaking until he had turned in at the gate with a flutter of his long coat-tails in the spring wind.

"Faix, I wisht we all had the sharp teeth for our dinners that his riverence has now," laughed Dennis. " I 'll be bound he 's keen for it, honest man. 'T was to early mass over to White Mills he was, lavin' by break o' day, an' just comin' back an' they sent to him for poor Mary Sullivan that 's to be waked this night, God rest her; and he not home from the corp' house an' Mary just dead, but two women come screechin' for him to hurry, there was a shild to be christened waitin' in the church; 't was one o' Jerry Hannan's wife's, that wint into black fits an' it being two hours born. Then it was high mass he had. I saw him myself puttin' a hand to his head an' humpin' wit' his shoulders, an' he before the alther. 'T is a great dale o' worruk, so it is, for a man the age o' Father Ryan, may God help him!"

"I 'd think the Bishop 'ould give him some aid now. They could sind some young missioner for a while to White Mills. 'T is out of our own rights we do be, an' he to White Mills, day an' night wit' them French, an' one of us took hurt or dyin'. 'T is too far to White Mills intirely," protested John Mulligan.

"Well, b'ys, the road 's clear for us now, an' I 'll say that I 've got the match to Father Ryan's hunger in me own inside, 't is thrue for me. Coom, Pat, now, there 's no more gerrls! Get a move on you now, John, the fince is tired from ye!" And being thus suitably urged Dennis's companions started on their way. Dennis himself was a sturdy, middle-aged man, a teamster for the manufacturing company that had long ago gathered these Irish people into the staid and prosperous New England village. They had made a neighborhood by themselves, and were just now alarmed in their turn and disturbed by the presence of a few French Canadians, so thoroughly did they feel at home and believe in their rights to an adopted country. They meant to stay, at any rate, and jealously suspected their lively neighbors of only a temporary appropriation of citizenship that would take more than it gave. Dennis Call would have been a prosperous man and good citizen anywhere, with his soberness and thrift and decent notions; he was much respected by his fellow-townsfolk.

"Coom, now!" exclaimed Pat Finn, trying to keep step with his tall companions, "'Leg over leg, as the dog wint to Dover,'" he added cheerfully. "I might have been coaxing a ride home wit' Braley's folks, they had the one sate saved in the wagon, but I was idlin' me time away wit' the likes of you; a taste of tark is always the ruin of me."

"Good-day to ye, Pat," the others called after him as he crossed over to go down a side-street; but the droll, stooping figure did not turn again, and Mulligan and Dennis went on in the peaceful company. Dennis was a step ahead of his friend. You rarely see the old-fashioned Irish folk walk side by side; perhaps they keep a dim remembrance of footpaths over the open fields and moors. There is less of the formal, military sense than belongs to most Europeans, and a coustant suggestion of the flock rather than the platoon.

At this moment two women who had lingered in the church overtook our friends and gave them a cordial greeting. One was the niece of Dennis Call, and almost as old as he. They lived at opposite ends of the town, and she stopped to ask him some questions about his family, while the other two, after hesitating a moment, went their way together. Sunday is the great social occasion for women who are hardly out of their houses all the rest of the week, and Dennis eagerly besought the favor of a visit. "Run home wit' me now for a bite of dinner," he urged. " 'T will be pot-luck, but the folks 'll give you a grand welcome, and some of the children will be coming to vespers."

"Yirra now, I can't then, Dinny," the niece insisted, but her face shone with gratification, and they both knew that she was ready to accept.

"Oh, be friendly now an' come an' see the folks," Dennis continued. "The poor woman was in all the week wit' a bad wakeness that troubles her very bad, 't is the stomach-bone falls down, they all says, but the docther has it that she 's only wantin' a bit of strength

wit' the spring weather an' all. 'T is a dale
o' work she has all the time, but the little
gerrls begins to help iligant now, an' 't will
soon be aisy; they grow very fast. Little
Mag is getting a foine dinner the day.
Coom, Mary!"

Mary gave a sigh of compassion for the
hard-worked mother, whose tiredness she
well comprehended. "You 're lucky then,
Dinnis, and herself is lucky, the two of you
bein' together and you gettin' steady work
the year through. I know well herself gets
a bit of the pain in her, we all gets it, faix!
I knows well what it is. 'T is our folks has
hard times, wid my man dead this sivin years
gone an' the old 'oman always in her bed,
an' I havin' to tind poor Johnny an' herself
like two babies. Wisha, wisha! I was n't
to mass — to-day is four Sundays gone since
I heard mass before. Well now, see! I 'm
goin' wid you like a little lost dog. I 'm
glad of a treat — but I 'll help little Mag wid
the dinner, so I will, 't is a task for the
shild."

A lovely readiness to help shone in Mary
O'Donnell's homely face. She looked poor
and anxious; her bonnet, with its brown and
white plaided ribbon and ancient shape,

looked as if it might have been ten years in wear. She had worn her poor mourning threadbare and returned to this headgear of an earlier and more prosperous time. She had been full of hope and cheerfulness when she bought the queer old brown bonnet, but a blessed light of hope and kindliness still shone in her eyes.

As they went along, busy with their homely talk, some one lifted a window near them and called " Dennis, Dennis!" in a tone of mild authority.

" 'T is his riverence wants you!" exclaimed Mrs. O'Donnell, flushing with excitement and pleasure. " I'll be going on slow; do you take your time. Run now, Dinny!"

" I'll be there, sir," said Dennis, already inside the gate, and by the time he reached the steps, Father Ryan opened the door. "Step in," he said; "I must have a word with you. Who's that with you?"

" Mary O'Donnell, she that's brother's-daughter to me, sir; 't ain't often we gets the bit of tark. She's goin' home to dinner with the folks, — herself's at home the day, sir, she's not well."

" I'll stop an' see her one day soon. I missed her at mass. Your wife's a good woman, Dennis."

"An' Mary O'Donnell, too, has done fine— she was afther bein' left very poor, 't is yourself knows it well, an' has been very kind, sir. She had but the two hands of her for depindence, but we all did what we could." Dennis had blushed at the priest's good words about his wife as if he himself had been praised. "I thank God I 'm prospered wit' good health, sir."

The old priest stood still in the narrow entry looking at Dennis Call as if he were not listening and were lost in his own thoughts. Dennis stood with hat in hand; the moment was strangely embarrassing. Father Ryan's strong-featured, good-humored face looked drawn and bluish as if he were really suffering from hunger and fatigue and some unforeseen perplexity beside. There was a cheerful insistent clatter of plates in the little dining-room beyond, and a comforting odor of roast-beef. Dennis felt more puzzled every moment, but he unconsciously smacked his lips in spite of uncertainties as to what the priest wanted.

"My heart 's sick, Dennis," said his reverence, and a sudden flicker of light shone in his eyes.

Dennis shifted his weight to the other foot

and passed his hat from right hand to left. "What's the matter, then, sir?" he asked anxiously. "Did anybody break the church window again I do' know?" He felt a little impatient; Mary O'Donnell would be far down the street, and the priest's good dinner made a man unbearably hungry. Still Father Ryan was frowning and planning without saying a word, and it made an honest man feel like a thief.

"Dennis, will you take a bit of dinner with me now and run afterward to Fletcher's place and get the best horse that's in, all in fifteen minutes' time? And say we're going on an errand of mercy if anybody puts a question. They'll think it's for the sick while it's for the well, God save us," said the old man.

"I'll do that, sir," said Dennis.

"Let's to dinner then," said Father Ryan. "I suppose good Mary O'Donnell's out of sound of your voice."

Dennis opened the door hastily, it was a relief to do something, and gave a loud call to Mary, who was still loitering not so very far away. "I'll not be home to my dinner," said he. "Do you go on then and tell the folks." So Mary, in happy amaze, went her ways to carry the pleasing news that Dennis was kept to his dinner with the priest.

Father Ryan was already in the dining-room; the roast-beef was smoking on the table, there were onions and potatoes, and even cranberry-sauce from some secret repository of the housekeeper, who was not unmindful of the priest's long morning of hard service. Mrs. Dillon was setting another plate opposite Father Ryan's own. Dennis forgot that he was clinging to his Sunday hat, but when they had blessed themselves, and dinner was fairly begun, and the hat pushed under the table, the guest felt that he could hold his own again, and ventured a sociable remark. Dennis was as quick as he could be, but the priest finished his beef first, and impatiently waved back a noble Sunday pudding which Mrs. Dillon was proudly bringing in at the door. "Run for the mare now, if you've had enough," said he, and Dennis gave a lingering glance at the pudding and departed.

"Lord be good to us, but he's in the hurry!" he grumbled, as he went at a jog trot down the street. It was not yet one o'clock and a lovely May afternoon. The season was early, and the maples in full leaf;

the prospect of a drive out into the country, with a light buggy, and possibly Fletcher's best mare, delighted Dennis Call as if he were a schoolboy. He marched into the stable yard with most important manners, and said, in the hearing of a group of stay-at-home loungers, that Father Ryan called for the best team and was in great haste.

"What's up, Dennis, a christening?" inquired an amiable idler; but Dennis plunged his hands deep into his pockets and calmly turned away, and looked up at the blue sky with an air of assurance, exactly as if he were not wishing that he knew, himself. Presently he stepped into the light carriage with the air of a lord, and whirled out of the yard.

"Which way now, sir?" he asked the priest, who was already waiting at his gate, but Father Ryan took the reins himself. "I'm afraid you might go too slow for me," he said, trying to give Dennis a droll, reassuring look, but he could not hide the provocation, and even grief, that he evidently felt. "I don't forget that you are used to heavy teaming," he added, and they both laughed and felt much more at ease. "I must be back in time for vespers," said his reverence, as they passed the church.

The sorrel mare sped along the road; her master had kept her in for his own use later that afternoon, and she was only too fresh and ready. For a while they followed the main road toward the next large town, and passed many of their acquaintances, driving or on foot, and Dennis was not without pride at being seen in the priest's company; but suddenly they turned into a rough, seldom-traveled by-way, that led up among the hills. It seemed as if the errand were to some person in trouble, but presently they had left behind what appeared to be the last house. This was a strange path to follow, and for what reason had Father Ryan desired a companion, unless it were necessary in such a steep and almost dangerous ascent? Once, years before, Dennis had climbed by this deserted road, up to the woodlands of the higher hills; he had been gunning with some young men, and he remembered the small, lonely farms that they had just passed, and how poor and inhospitable they looked in the winter weather; in fact, his remembrance of the holiday was not bright in any way, because he had gained but a poor day's sport. None of the priest's flock lived in this direction, that was one sure thing.

The road seemed to grow steeper and steeper; the sorrel mare stopped once or twice, discouraged, and looked ahead at the hard climb. There were dark hemlocks and pines on either side, illuminated here and there by the vivid green of young birch saplings that stood where they caught the sunlight. The air was fresh and sweet, there were busy birds fluttering and calling; the light tread of the mare seemed to disturb the secluded region, as if nothing had passed that way since the coming of the year.

Father Ryan had not spoken for a long time; all the cheerfulness had faded from his face. "Dennis!" said he suddenly, so that the man at his side turned, startled and open-eyed, to look at him. "Dennis, you remember that smart young Dan Nolan, Tom Nolan's boy, the one that went to the seminary for a while, but left and went West to be a railroad man?"

"I does mind Danny Nolan, sir; they say he's got rich. Him an' John Finnerty's gerrl is courtin' this long time, the pritty gerrl Katy; I saw her coming out from mass the day. John Finnerty do be thinking she's got a great match, the b'y always says in his letters that he's doing fine."

"May God forgive him!" said the priest, under his breath.

"Why, in course I'd know him well, sir," Dennis continued eagerly, in his most communicative manner. "Wasn't he brought up next house to my own by the mill yard, until I moved to the better one I'm in now, thanks be to God, the other one being dacint to look at, but very damp an' the cause of much sickness to every one. Oh, but the fine letters the b'y does be writing home, they brings them and reads them to herself an' me; truth is Tom Nolan's put his money into a mine that Danny's knowing to, out where he is, and they've been at me would n't I come wid 'em. Every one says there do be a power o' money in it. The tark is all right, but for Tom not having got any papers; I'd like to see the papers they gives, first; an' I think meself, sir, it's the same with Tom, but he won't let on."

"My God!" said the old priest again.

"An' John Finnerty, the little gerrl's fadther, he sint t'ree hundred — 't was all he had laid by — you know the wife's a great spinder — an' Danny Nolan wrote back he'd find it t'ree thousand this time next year, an' herself has been in the street goin' to the

shops ivery night since then, as rich-feeling
as a conthractor! Katy, the young thing,
sint him out her small savings she got in the
mill that she was keeping to buy her wedding
with. I was against that when they tould
me, but she'd sint to Dan and he wrote a
great letter to sind it along, an' he'd put it
where it would grow. 'Too many eggs in
the one basket,' says I. She's awful proud
of Dan, and he do be always writin' the
beautiful letters, sir; but he does be knowing
his fadther works hard all the time, and at
Christmas last year divil a cint came home to
any one of them. They all says it was too far
entirely to be gettin' prisents, but they'd like
to be showing anything they got the lingth
of the town. Tell me now, sir, do ye know
of anything wrong? I do be thinkin' you've
heard bad news. I could n't tell why" —

Father Ryan touched the horse and gave
a queer groan before he spoke.

"The truth is that Dan Nolan's a swin-
dler," said he. "Those poor souls 'll never
see their money again."

"Well, something held me back from
him, thanks be to God!" protested Dennis
with pride, though he looked shocked and
anxious. "I come very near givin' him all

I had too. Whin a craze gets amongst folks, one must be doing like all the rest; ain't it so, sir? And that Dan was the best scholar in the schools here; don't you mind the praise he 'd get from every one, an' his fadther was proud as a paycock. I does be thinkin' them schools has their faults. If a man dies now an' laves a houseful of childher they don't be half so fit to earn their bread as they were in the old times. I 'm thinkin' the old folks was wiser wit' the childher, Father Ryan, sir!"

"There never was a boy in any parish I had these forty-five years that I took the pains with that I took with him," said Father Ryan slowly. "I paid the most of his bills myself when he went to the seminary. Poor Tom Nolan could n't do it, with his small wages and the sickness and the trouble he used to have. Danny was my altar-boy, — a pretty face there was on him, and a laughing eye. He always stood to me for a little brother of mine, and looked the very marrow of him when I first saw him, and Tom came to the mills. My little brother was my playmate, we were always together like twin lambs. I can mind myself now, and I running home alone, crying, to tell my poor mother that we 'd run away to the rocks, and a great wave came in and licked him off before my very eyes, and I a bit higher up on the shore. I wake up dreaming of him, stiff with the horror and a cold sweat all over me, after a lifetime that 's gone between me and that day. I 'm an old man now, Dennis Call, and my mind 's always been in a priest's holy business. But I 've a warm Irish heart in me, and there are times when I 'd like a brother's young child, or one of my sister's that I left long ago in Kerry, or to see my old mother shake her head and have the laugh at me, and I sitting there in the long winter evening in my still house. And when that young Danny Nolan gave a smile at me, like the little lad that went under the sea, and never was afraid, or trying to get away from me because I was the priest, I liked him more than I knew. I could n't see then why he should n't make a good man, and I helped him the best I could. I know plenty of harm of him now, God forgive him and bring him to repentance."

The old man scowled and looked away. His heart was filled with sorrow. Dennis's ready tongue was checked, but he was grumbling to himself about the black heart of Danny Nolan. "I begin to think that sharp wits are the least of all the means by which a man wins true success," said Father Ryan.

"Everybody thought well of Dan Nolan then, sir." Dennis tried to comfort him; he had seen Father Ryan angry and stern, but never cast down like this.

They came to an open, grassy space on a shelf of the great hill. At one side was the cellar where a house had stood long ago; some roses still grew about it, and there was much of the solemn little cypress plant, so often seen in country burying-grounds, growing about the crumbling foundations and straying off into the grass. There was a smooth, broad doorstep partly overgrown, and a hop-vine was sending up its determined shoots near by, where it could find nothing to twine upon. The old doorstep had evidently served as a seat for stray wanderers; there was a place before it that had been worn by feet, like the beginning of a path. The house had been gone many years, but one might have thought that its ghost was there, and the doorstep was still trodden by those unseen inhabitants who went and came. The priest may have thought this, but Dennis saw a gun wad lying by the step, and a little bird fluttered away, as if it had been finding a few stray crumbs.

There was a magnificent view of the wide-spread lower country — woods and clearings and bushy pasture-lands stretching miles upon miles, with a river dividing them like a shining ribbon; and white villages, with their tiny spires and sprinkled houses and heavy dark mills. As you turned the other way you looked up the dark hill-slope. The road appeared to end here by the deserted farmstead, but some winter wood-roads led off in different directions.

Father Ryan stopped the breathless mare and got down clumsily. "We'll walk from here, Dennis," he said, and Dennis also alighted. His face was befogged with perplexity. They plunged deep into the woods along one of the half overgrown winter tracks which led up and over a high shoulder of the great hill.

"'T is like the way to the cave of the foxy 'oman," said Dennis, half aloud, as a dry twig whipped him in the face, and Father Ryan heard him and laughed.

" Well, it's wonderful how those old tales

do stay in the mind," he said cheerfully. "I was working away with a book yesterday, a fine hard knot of Latin it was, too, and I got sleepy, and not a bit could I think of but how did the story of the Little Cakeen go that my old granny used to tell me before she'd give me a little cakeen herself that she'd have hidden in her blue cloak. I'd be afraid to eat it, too, after the tale. Well, I think it might be twenty years since I thought of it, but I could not rid my mind of the trick of that foolish story, and it kept twirling itself round and round in my mind. It may be the way with old folks. I begin to feel old."

" 'T was a great story of the Little Cakeen," agreed Dennis solemnly. "I do be telling it to the childher; there's nothing anybody tells that they'd like so well, wit' their little screeches always in the same place. 'T was the same way wit' my brothers and meself at home. We'd better mind, sir, lest ourselves gets on the fox's back an' into his big mout'. Do you know where you do be going?" Dennis looked about him anxiously.

The priest only laughed; a queer laugh it was that might mean one thing or another.

"Come on!" he said. "You make me think of another old tale they used to be telling at home about one Mrs. O'Flaherty's donkey, that could neither go nor stand still."

At this moment, when the conversation had taken a most sociable and even merry tone, the two men found themselves on the edge of the thick woods, with an open, partly overgrown acre of land before them. The seedling pines had covered a piece of land cleared and deserted again many years before; they had grown close to the tumble-down old house, which had sometimes been used as a shelter by lumbermen who were at work among the hills, or sportsmen who might have taken refuge there in wet weather. Dennis was astonished to find himself there; he remembered the place well, but they had reached it by so short a path that the priest seemed to have brought him by the aid of magic. Dennis had taken heart at a change for the better in Father Ryan's manner, and was already preparing to laugh at the expected story about a donkey; but Father Ryan looked stern and priestly again and began to stride forward, telling Dennis by a gesture to wait outside the house. "'T is a den of thieves I 'm sure, now," muttered Dennis, but he followed his companion to the door, and stood there, strong and sturdy and not displeased, looking about him suspiciously like a wary sentinel.

The priest stepped softly on the pasture turf among the little pine-trees, and entered the door as if he did not mean to be heard. Immediately there was a scuffle and crash inside and the jar of a heavy fall, at which Dennis Call rushed in with his eyes dancing and his fists clenched.

There, in the middle of the dismal rain-stained room, by an overturned table and broken chair, Father Ryan was fighting with a younger man and getting the worst of it. Dennis pounced down and caught the fellow off by the shoulders. His great thumbs held down the cords like iron bolts; he stood the rascal back on his knees and gave him a terrible shaking. Dennis had been a tidy man at a fight when he was younger, and his rage revived the best of his experience. "Get up, sir; get up, your riverence!" he commanded, in a bold voice. "Lave the beggar to me!" and he kept his clutch with one hand while he administered a succession of sound blows with the other. "Take that, will you now, Danny Nolan, an' that wit' it!" he said scornfully. "Is it full of drink you are, I do' know, to strike down an old an' rispicted man that's been a fadther to you, and he God's priest beside! I'll bate the life out of you and lave you here to the crows an' I get a saucy word out o' your head, so there, now!" and Dennis proceeded to cuff and shake his captive unmercifully.

The old priest looked shocked and shaken; he got upon his feet and tried to brush the dust from his black clothes. There was no place to sit, it was a dirty, stifling place, and he turned and went swaying with faltering steps to the door, and Dennis, holding the young man's arm in an unflinching grip, went after him.

"Sit down on the step, sir," he said, anxiously, to the old man. "I hope it is n't faint you are, sir?"

Father Ryan seated himself upon the crumbling door-sill, and Dennis backed himself and his captive against a bowlder that stood in front of the old house, close by. As he turned to take a good look at Dan Nolan, a feeling of contempt stolé into his honest face. In the clear light the young man looked so colorless and disreputable, wrecked and ruined by an only too evident life of vice and ignorance of every sort of decent behavior, that he seemed but a poor antagonist for a man like Dennis Call. There was little left of his boyish good looks and fine spirit. He must have thrown Father Ryan by some trick that caught him unprepared, for in spite of his age the priest looked much the stronger of the two. Dennis felt a strange anxiety as he saw how badly out of breath Father Ryan was still, and what bad color had come to his lips.

"Will I get you a sup of water, sir?" he asked eagerly. "This thing 'ont run away; or I'll just stun the poor cr'ature a bit wit' me fist so he can't step foot an' he tries. I'm afraid you're bad off, sir, so I am."

"No, no," said Father Ryan. "Let go his arm now."

"I don't dare lave him go, sir," protested Dennis.

"Let go his arm. Stand out, Dan!" and a strange light blazed in the old man's eyes. Danny Nolan, in his smart, dirty, city-made clothes, stood out a step in front of Dennis, a poor wretched image of a young man as ever startled the squirrels and jays of that wild, deserted bit of country. He cast a furtive glance to the right and left, but the old priest raised a warning hand.

" No, you won't run, Dan, my boy," he said. " My old heart is ready to break at the sorry sight of you. Those poor legs of yours would throw you before you could run a rod. Take out the money that 's in your pockets. Dennis, keep your eye on him now. Take it out, I say ! "

Father Ryan rose to his great height with a black and angry look; his years seemed to fall off his shoulders like a cloak, and Dennis stepped forward eager for the fray. The fellow was at bay. He looked for a moment as sharp and ugly as a weasel, then the cowardice in him showed itself; he began to whimper and weaken, and so fell upon his knees.

" It is in the state's prison that you ought to be. I know it well," said Father Ryan sternly.

" Will I give him a nate kick or two, your riverence ? " inquired Dennis suggestively. " May be 't will help him to mind what you do be saying, the dirty bla'guard."

Danny Nolan, still whimpering, took something from his pocket and dropped it before him on the turf. "There, now," he said, trying to be bold, "let me go."

"Go through his pockets yourself, Dennis," said the priest, and he stood watching while this business was carefully accomplished, and a little heap of counterfeit bills was gathered at their feet, which Dennis had sought for with little tenderness. "What have you hidden in the house beside?" he demanded, looking up in black rage, as Danny Nolan stood there, surly and flushed.

"If 't was my last word, I 'd tell you the same," he answered. "There 's no more but this. I was only waiting till evening, so I 'd get away. There 's two dollars there that 's good," he sulkily added, touching the money with his foot.

"Ye 'd best give it to his riverence for a collection, then," Dennis advised. "Ain't you the dirthy divil!"

"I 've had awful hard luck," said Danny, in a grieved tone. "'T was a man on the cars give me this" —

"Why did n't you come straight to those who were your friends?" said Father Ryan sadly. "You have been robbing those that loved you and taking their little earnings —

you are a liar and a thief. How will you face them now and go to them for food and shelter? Who 'll want to give you a day's work? You have been living with cheats and liars; see what they have done for you, and how rich and fine you come home to those that have praised you the length of the town. What do you mean to do?"

"They 're out after me; the officers are out after me, sir." The poor rascal instantly turned to his old friend for help. "I can't stop here; 't was the man that gave me this stuff to get rid of it himself, and then went and told."

"You sent down to the mills to some fellows you thought bad enough to buy this trash. Don't lie to me, Dan! You have fallen into this sort of thing by your own choice. Come now, if Dennis and I will stand by you, will you try to be decent and live honest? You 'll be dead this time next year if you don't, and there 's God's truth for you. I 'll try you this once more, God helping me. I 'll not send you home to those that are n't able to keep you. I 've a little money put by, and I 'll lend you something for those you have robbed and cheated with your stories about the mine."

"I was cheated myself in the first place, Father Ryan," said Nolan. Then he fell to sobbing and covered his face with both his hands. "I've been bad, you're right, sir, but oh, try me again. I don't know what'll I do. I'm starved here, and every bush that rustles turns me cold these three nights. I'll do the best I can, sir. I wouldn't have said it so easy yesterday, but I'm beat to the ground now. Everybody's turned against me. I thought some friends of mine would be here last night" —

"Come, stand up an' behave like a man!" Dennis gave him a vigorous jerk by way of stimulant. "We mane no harm by the likes of you. Do now as Father Ryan says, since he's so willing to try you." There was kindliness in his tone, though the shake was contradictory. "I'll stand by you meself for Father Ryan's pleasure, but it goes hard wit' me to say the word."

"You'll come to me this evening at eight o'clock," said the priest. "I'll be thinking what's best to do. I can't stand between you and the laws you've broken. You'll stay at my house the night. Mrs. Dillon 'll be washing in the morning; the first thing is to make you look decent. Then I'll find a way to talk with your father, poor honest man!"

"I'd as soon go chop at Tom Nolan wit' me ax," muttered Dennis.

The priest stooped and struck a match on the gray rock and touched it to the counterfeit bills, stirring them now and then with his foot as they smouldered. When the few ashes began to blow in the light spring wind, and there was little left but an ugly small scar in the green turf, Father Ryan held out his hand and Danny Nolan tried not to see it and turned away. The old priest could not help a sigh. Then the young man, who had known every sin, threw himself upon the mercy of this merciful old friend. No matter if Dennis stood by with his aggravating sense of honesty, his narrow experience of a stupid mill town, Dan Nolan caught hold of Father Ryan's hand and clung to it as if his whole heart were spent in love and gratitude. "O God, help me; I'll not fail you this night, sir. 'T is the Lord sent you to me, sir. 'T is you were always good to me when I was a little boy minding the altar, sir."

"You were always great wit' your fine words and your smart letters," grumbled

Dennis, who in spite of himself was much affected. If his own sons should ever go wrong, God send them such a friend. " See now that you give his riverence satisfaction for all the trouble he 's taking, and pay him back his money too. There 's work enough if you 'd only be dacint, but if I 'd hear from any of your tricks, or you 'd be doing harm among the young folks, Lord be good to me but I 'd be the one to break your neck, so I would. When I think of that pritty gerrl you 've fooled ! " —

" Don't shame the man any more. We 'll give him his chance to do better. 'T is God does the same every day for you and me," said Father Ryan.

The May wind in the pine woods was like the sound of the sea as the two elder men turned away to go down the hill, not once looking back. The old priest left Dan Nolan behind as if he had forgotten him, and Dennis was awed into speechlessness as he walked alongside.

The sorrel mare was restless. She had unwisely browsed the sharp-thorned sprouting rosebushes, and had got the reins tangled about her feet. Father Ryan climbed into the carriage; he began to feel lame and tired, and Dennis, still silent, took the mare by the head and led her carefully down the steepest part of the road. When they came to the lowest slope of the hill he got in and took the reins, and they went quickly home. The church-bells began to ring for vespers as they neared the town.

"I 'll be a trifle late, I 'm sorry," said the priest. "Leave me at the church and you go on with the mare, Denny. Oh, I 'm all right, 't was fine and pleasant in the green woods. It seems long to me since mass was over."

"My saints in heaven, but ain't he the father to us!" exclaimed Dennis, a moment later. He still felt a delightful sense of excitement and adventure, but after they had parted at the church something choked him, as he thought of Father Ryan's figure as he had seen him go along the little path to the vestry, with that dust on the back of his coat. As he came back to the church himself he overtook Mary O'Donnell, who greeted him with pleasure and even curiosity, and some other friends made mention of the fact that he had been away with the priest. The parishioners were used to being ignorant about most of Father Ryan's affairs; a priest could never make talk about his errands of business and mercy as another man could.

The warm May Sunday indeed seemed long. The vesper service did not often attract Dennis Call. He was always in his place at mass, but he took his Sunday sleep and stroll in the afternoon. He made himself easy in the corner of the pew, he picked some pine-needles out of the cuff of his coat, and he said, a little grudgingly, a prayer for Danny Nolan. He noticed that there was a bruise beginning to show itself on the old priest's forehead, and how the hands trembled that were lifted at the altar. The doctor had been known to say that Father Ryan was not a sound man, that he had better not take long walks alone any more, or overtax himself as he often did, and Dennis wondered vaguely if this were not the reason he had been called upon that day for company.

"I'd like to clout the saucy bla'guard a couple o' times more," he grumbled to himself; but his heart was not without compassion. His own boys were just beginning to put on the airs and to share the ambitions of men, and poor Tom Nolan, his old friend and neighbor, must hear sad news of Danny, and that soon. Dennis blinked his sleepy eyes and looked reverently at Father Ryan's tall figure at the altar. The setting sun brought out the color and tarnished gold thread of the worn vestments. The paper flowers that a French woman had made new at Easter looked gay and almost real in the pleasant light.

" 'T is in many strange places that a priest does be having to serve God," said Dennis to himself. " I 'm thinking Danny Nolan 'll light out this night wit' the two dollars, an' we 'll see no more of him. Faix, 't would be best for him, the young fool; the likes of him will break every heart, stay or go!"

That night, however, just at dark, Dan Nolan came across the fields, and presently stole out from a thicket at the foot of the priest's little garden, and went into the house. The lights were bright; there was a good supper on the table. As the hungry, crestfallen offender sat there, abashed by all the light and good cheer, the old man's tired face shone with golden hopefulness. Father Ryan even persuaded himself that the look of his own young brother had come back again into Danny Nolan's eyes.

A LITTLE CAPTIVE MAID.

I.

THE early winter twilight was falling over the town of Kenmare; a heavy open carriage with some belated travelers bounced and rattled along the smooth highway, hurrying toward the inn and a night's lodging. Two slender young figures drew back together into the leafless hedge by the roadside and stood there, whispering and keeping fast hold of hands after the simple fashion of children and lovers. There was an empty bird's nest close beside them, and they looked at that, and after they had watched the carriage a moment, and even laughed because Dinny Killoren, the driver, had recognized their presence by a loud snap of his whip, they still loitered. The girl turned away from her lover, who only looked at her, and felt the soft lining of the nest with the fingers of her left hand. Johnny Morris's handsome young face looked pinched and sad in the gray dampness of the dusk.

"The poor tidy cr'atures!" said Nora Connelly. "Look now at their little house, Johnny, how nate it is, and they gone from it. I mind the birds singing in the hedge one day last summer, and I walking by in the road."

"Wisha, 't is our own tidy house I 'm thinking of," said Johnny reproachfully; "I 've long dramed of it, and now whatever will I do and you gone away to Ameriky? Faix, it 's too hard for us, Norry dear; we 'll get no luck from your goin'; 't was the Lord mint us for aich other!"

"I 'm safe to come back, darling," said Nora, troubled by her lover's lamentations. "'T is for the love of you I 'm going, sure, Johnny dear! I suppose 't is yourself won't want me then aither, when I come back; sure they says folks dries all up there, and gets brown and small wit' the heat that 's in it. Promise now that you 'll say nothing sharp, so long as I 'm fine an' rich coming home!"

"Don't break me heart, Nora, wit' your wild talk; who else but yourself would be joking, and our hearts breaking wit' parting, and this our last walk together," mourned the young man. "Come, darling, we must be going on. 'T is a good way yet through the town, an' your aunt 's ready to have my life now for not sinding you back at t'ree o'clock."

"Let her wait!" said Nora scornfully. "I 'll be free of her, then, this time to-morrow. 'T is herself 'll be keenin' after me as if 't was wakin' me she was, and the cold heart of stone that 's inside her and no tears to her eyes. They might be glass buttons in her old head, they might then! I 'd love you to the last day I lived, John Morris, if 't was only to have the joke on her;" and Nora's eyes sparkled with fun. "I 'd spite her if I could, the old crow! Sorra a bit of lave-takin' have I got from her yet, but to say I must sind home my passage-money inside the first month I 'm out. Oh, but, Johnny, I 'll be so lonesome there; 't is a cold home I had since me mother died, but God help me when I 'm far from it!" The girl and her lover were both crying now; Johnny kissed her and put his arms tenderly about her, there where they stood alone by the roadside; both knew that the dreaded hour of parting had come.

Presently, as if moved by the stern hand of fate rather than by their own will, they

walked away along the road, still weep-
ing. They came into the town, where lights
were bright in the houses. There was the
usual cheerful racket about the inn. The
Lansdowne Arms seemed to be unusually
populous and merry for a winter night.
Somebody called to Johnny Morris from a
doorway, but he did not answer. Close by
were the ruins of the old abbey, and he drew
Nora with him between the two stones which
made a narrow entrance-way to the grounds.
It was dreary enough there among the wintry
shadows, the solemn shapes of the crumbling
ruin, and the rustling trees.

"Tell me now once more that you love
me, darling," sobbed the poor lad; "you 're
goin' away from me, Nora, an' 't is you 'll
find it aisy to forget. Everything you lave
will be speakin' to me of you. Oh, Nora,
Nora! howiver will I lave you go to Ameriky! I was no man at all, or why did n't
I forbid it? 'T is only I was too poor to
keep you back, God help me! *O Dea! O
Dea!*"

"Be quiet now," said Nora. "I 'll not forget you. I 'll save all my money till I 'll
come back to you. We 're young, dear lad,
sure; kiss me now an' say good-by, my fine

gay lad, and then walk home quiet wit' me
through the town. I call the holy saints to
hear me that I won't forget."

And so they kissed and parted, and walked
home quiet through the town as Nora had
desired. She stopped here and there for a
parting word with a friend, and there was
even a sense of dignity and consequence in
the poor child's simple heart because she was
going to set forth on her great journey the
next morning, while others would ignobly
remain in Kenmare. Thank God, she had
no father and mother to undergo the pain
of seeing her disappear forever from their
eyes. The poor heart-broken Irish folk who
let their young sons and daughters go away
from them to America, — which of us has
stopped half long enough to think of their
sorrows and to pity them? What must it
be to see the little companies set forth on
their way to the sea, knowing that they will
return no more? The fever for emigration
is a heart-rending sort of epidemic, and the
boys and girls who dream of riches and pleasure until they are impatient of their homes in
poor, beautiful Ireland! alas, they sail away
on the crowded ships to find hard work and
hard fare, and know their mistakes about

finding a fairy-land too late, too late! And Nora Connelly's aunt had hated Johnny Morris, and laid this scheme for separating them, under cover of the furtherance of Nora's welfare. They had been lovers from their childhood, and Johnny's mother, from whom Nora had just parted on that last sad evening, was a sickly woman and poor as poverty. Johnny was like son and daughter both, he could never leave her while she lived; they had needed all of Nora's cheerfulness and love, and now they were going to lose her, perhaps forever. Everybody knew how few come back from America; no wonder that these Irish hearts were sad with parting.

On the morrow there was little time for leave-takings. Some people tried to make it a day of jokes and festivities when such parties of emigrants left the country-side, but there was always too much sadness underneath the laughter; and the chilly rain fell that day as if Ireland herself wept for her wandering children, — poor Ireland, who gives her best to the great busy countries over seas, and longs for the time when she can be rich and busy herself, and keep the young people at home and happy in field and town. What does the foreign money cost that comes back to the cottage households broken as if by death? What does it cost to the aching hearts of fathers and mothers, to the homesick lads and girls in America, with the cold Atlantic between them and home?

II.

The winter day was clear and cold, with a hint of coming spring in the blue sky. As you came up Barry Street, the main thoroughfare of a thriving American town, you could not help noticing the thick elm branches overhead, and the long rows of country horses and sleighs before the stores, and a general look of comfortably mingled country and city life.

The high-storied offices and warehouses came to an end just where the hill began to rise, and on the slope, to the left, was a terraced garden planted thick with fruit-trees and flowering shrubbery. Above this stood a large, old-fashioned white house close to the street. At first sight one was pleased with its look of comfort and provincial elegance,

but as you approached, the whole lower
story seemed unused. If you glanced up at
a window of the second story, you were likely
to see an elderly gentleman looking out, pale
and unhappy, as if invalidism and its en-
forced idleness were peculiarly hard for him
to bear. Sometimes you might catch sight
of the edge of a newspaper, but there was
never a book in his hand, there was never
a child's face looking out to companion the
old man. People always spoke of poor old
Captain Balfour nowadays, but only a few
months before, he had been the leading business man of the city, absorbed in a dozen
different enterprises. A widower and child-
less, he felt himself to be alone indeed in this
time of illness and despondency. Early in
life he had followed the sea, from choice, not
necessity, but for many years he had been
master of the old house and garden on Barry
Street, his inherited home. People always
spoke of him with deference and respect,
they pitied him now in his rich and pitiful
old age. In the early autumn a stroke of
paralysis had dulled and disabled him, and
its effect was more and more puzzling, and
irritating beside to the captain's pride.

He more and more insisted upon charging

his long captivity and uncomfortable condition at the doors of his medical advisers and the household. At first, in dark and gloomy weather, or in days of unusual depression, a running fire of comments was kept up toward those who treated him like a child, and who made an apothecary's shop of his stomach, and kept him upon such incomprehensible diet. A slice of salt beef and a captain's biscuit were indignantly demanded at these times, but it was touching to observe that the person in actual attendance was always treated with extreme consideration or even humble gratitude, while the offenders were always absent. " *They* " were guilty of all the wrongs and kept the captain miserable; *they* were impersonal foes of his peace; there never was anything but a kind word for Mrs. Nash, the housekeeper, or Reilly, the faithful attendant; there never were any personal rebukes administered to the cook; and as for the doctor, Captain Balfour treated him as one gentleman should treat another.

Until early in January, when once in a while even the hitherto respected Mrs. Nash was directly accused of a total lack of judgment, and James Reilly could not do or say anything to suit, and the lives of these honest persons became nearly unbearable; the maid under Mrs. Nash's charge (for the household had always been kept up exactly as in Mrs. Balfour's day) could not be expected to consider the captain's condition and her own responsibilities as his older and deeply attached companions could, and, tired of the dullness and idleness of the old house, fell to that state where dismissal was inevitable. Then neither Mrs. Nash nor Reilly knew what to do next; they were not as young as they had been, and, to use their own words, minded the stairs. At last Reilly, a sensible man, proposed a change in the order of housekeeping. The captain might never come downstairs any more; they could shut up the dining-room and the parlors, and make their daily work much lighter.

"An' I won't say that I have n't got word for you of a tidy little girl," said Reilly, beseechingly. "She 's a relation to my cousins the Donahues, and as busy as a sparrow. She 'll work beside you an' the cook like your own shild, she will that, Mrs. Nash, and is a light-hearted shild the day through. She 's just over too, the little greenhorn!"

"Perhaps she 'll be just what we want, Reilly," agreed the housekeeper, after reflection. "Send her up to see me this very evening, if you're going where she is."

So the very next day, into the desolate old house came young Nora Connelly, a true child of the old country, with a laughing gray eye and a smooth girlish cheek, and a pretty touch of gold at the edge of the fair brown hair about her forehead. It was a serious little face, not beautiful, except in its delightful girlishness. She was a friendly, kindly little creature, fond of her simple pleasures, and willing to work hard the day through. The great house itself was a treasure-house of new experience, and she felt her position in the captain's family to be a valued promotion.

One morning, life looked very dark to the master. Everything had been going wrong since breakfast, and the captain rang for Reilly when he had just gone out, and Mrs. Nash was busy with a messenger.

"Go up, will you, Nora?" she said anxiously, "and say that I'll be there in a minute. Reilly's just left him."

And Nora sped away, nothing loath; she had never taken a satisfactory look at the master, and this was the fourth day since she had come to the house.

She opened the door and saw a handsome, fretful, tired old gentleman, whose newspaper had slipped from his hand and gone out of reach. She hurried to pick it up, without being told.

"Who are you?" inquired the captain, looking at her with considerable interest.

"Nora Connelly, sir," said the girl in a delicious Irish voice. "I'm your new maid, sir, since Winsday. I feel very sorry for your bein' ill, sir."

"There's nothing the matter with me," growled the captain unexpectedly.

"Wisha, sir, I'm glad of that!" said Nora, with a wag of her head like a bird, and a light in her eye. "Mrs. Nash'll be here at once, sir, for your ordhers. She is daling wit' a boy below in the hall. You are looking fine an' comfortable the day, sir."

"I never was so uncomfortable in my life," said the captain. "You can open that window."

"And it snowing fast, sir? You'll let out all the fine heat; heat's very dear now and cold is cheap, so it is, with poor folks. 'T is a great pity you've no turfs now to keep your fire in for you. 'T is very strange there do be no turf in this foine country;"

and she looked at the captain with a winning smile. The captain smiled back again in spite of himself.

Nora stood looking out of the window; she seemed to be thinking of herself instead of the invalid.

"What did you say your name was?" asked the old gentleman, a moment later, frowning his eyebrows at her like pieces of artillery.

"Plase, sir, I 'm Nora Connelly, from the outside o' Kenmare." She made him the least bit of a courtesy, as if a sudden wind had bent her like a long-stemmed flower.

"How came you here?" His mouth straightened into a smile as he spoke, in spite of a determination to be severe.

"I 'm but two weeks over, sir. I come over to me cousins, the Donahues, seeking me fortune. I 'd like Ameriky, 'tis a fine place, sir, but I 'm very homesick intirely. I 'm as fast to be going back as I was to be coming away;" and she gave a soft sigh and turned away to brush the hearth.

"Well, you must be a good girl," said the captain, with great propriety, after a pause.

" 'Deed, sir, I am that," responded Nora sincerely. "No one had a word to fling afther me and I coming away, but crying afther me. Nobody 'll tell anything to my shame when my name 'll be spoke at home. My mother brought me up well, God save her, she did, then!"

This unaffected report of her own good reputation was pleasing to Nora's employer; the sight of Nora's simple, pleasant Irish face and the freshness of her youth was the most delightful thing that had happened in many a dreary day. He felt in his waist-coat pocket with sudden impulse, sure of finding a bit of money there with which Nora Connelly might buy herself a ribbon. He was strongly inclined toward making her feel at home in the old house which had grown to be such a prison to himself. But there was no money in the pocket, as there always used to be when he was well. He had not needed any before in a long time. He began to fret about this, and to wonder what they had done with his pocket-book; it was ignominious to be treated like a school-boy. While he brooded over his wrongs, Nora heard Mrs. Nash's hurrying footsteps in the hall, but as she slipped away it was

plain that she had found time enough to be-
stow her entire sympathy, and even affection,
upon the captain in this brief interview.

"He 's dull, poor gentleman, — he 's very
sad all day by himself, and so pleasant spoken, the cr'ature!" she said to herself indignantly, as she went running down the stairs.

It was not long before, to everybody's
surprise, Captain Balfour gained strength,
and began to feel so much better that Nora
was often posted in the room or the hall close
by to run his frequent errands and pick up
his newspapers as they fell. This gave Mrs.
Nash and Reilly a chance to look after their
other business affairs, and to take their ease
after so long a season of close attendance.
The captain had a gruff way of asking,
"Where 's that little girl?" as if he only
wished to see her to scold roundly ; and Nora
was always ready to come with her sewing or
any bit of housework that could be carried,
and to entertain her master by the hour.
The more irritable his temper, the more unconscious and merry she always seemed.

"I was down last night wit' me cousins, so
I was," she informed him one morning, while
she brushed up the floor about the fireplace

on her hands and knees. " You 'd ought to see her little shild, sir; indade she 's the darling cr'ature. I never saw any one so crabbed and smart for the size of her. She ain't the heighth of a bee's knee, sir ! "

" Who is n't ? " inquired the captain absently, attracted for the moment by the pleasing simile.

" Me cousin's little shild, sir," answered Nora appealingly, with a fear that she had failed in her choice of a subject. " 'T is no more than the heighth of a bee's knee she is, the colleen, and has every talk to you like a little grandmother, — the big words of her haves to come sideways out of her mouth. I 'd like it well if her mother would dress her up prertty, and I 'd go fetch her for you to see."

The captain made an expressive sound of disdain, and Nora brushed away at the rug in silence. He looked out of the window and drummed on the arm of his chair. It was a very uncomfortable morning. There was a noise in the street, and Nora pricked up her ears with her head alert like a young hare, stood up on her knees, and listened.

" I 'll warrant it 's me heart's darling tooting at the fife," she exclaimed.

"Nothing but a parcel of boys," grumbled the captain.

"Faix it's he, then, the dacint lad!" said Nora, by this time close to the other front window. "Look at him now, sir, goin' by! He's alther-b'y in the church, and a lovely voice in him. Me cousins is going to have him learn music. That's 'The girl I left behind me,' he's got in the old fife now."

"Hard to tell what it is," growled the captain. "Anything for a racket, I dare say."

"Faix, sir, I was thinking meself the tune come out of it tail first," agreed Nora with ready sympathy. "He's the big brother to the little sisther I told you of just now. 'Twas Dan Sullivan gave Johnny the old fife; himself used to play it in a company. There's a kay or two gone, I'm misthrusting; anyway there's teeth gone in the tune."

Nora was again brushing the floor industriously. The captain was listless and miserable; the silence vexed him even more than the harmless prattle.

"I used to play the flute pretty well myself when I was a young man," he said pleasantly, after a while.

"I'd like well to hear you, then, sir," said Nora enthusiastically. She was only making an excuse of the brushing to linger with him a little while. "Oh, but your honor would have liked to hear me mother sing. God give her rest, but she had the lovely voice for you! They'd be sinding for her from three towns away to sing with the fiddle for weddings and dances. If you'd hear her sing the 'Pride of Glencoe' 't would take the heart out of you, it would indade."

"My wife was a most beautiful singer when she was young. I like to hear a pretty voice," said the captain sadly.

"'T was me dear mother had it, then," answered Nora. "I do be often minding her singing when I'm falling asleep. I hear her voice very plain sometimes. My mother was from the north, sir, and she had tunes that did n't be known to the folks about Kenmare. 'Inniskillen Dragoon' was one of the best liked, and it went lovely with the wheel when she'd be spinning. Everybody'd be calling for her to sing that tune. Strangers would come and ask her for a song that were passing through the town. There was great talk always of me mother's singing; they'd know of her for twinty miles round. Whin I see the fire gone down in red coals like this, like our turf at home, and it does be growing dark, I remimber well 't was such times she 'd sing like a bird for us, being through her long day's work, an' all of us round the fire kaping warm if we could, a winter night. Oh, but she 'd sing then like a lark in the fields, God rest her!"

Nora brushed away a tear and blessed herself. "You 'd like well to hear me mother sing, sir, I 'm telling you God's truth," she said simply. And the old captain watched her and smiled, as if he were willing to hear more.

"Folks would pay her well, too. They 'd all be afraid she 'd stop when she 'd once begin. There was nobody but herself could sing with the fiddle. I mind she came home one morning when she 'd been sint for to a great wedding, — 't was a man's only daughter that owned his own land. And me mother came home to us wit' a collection of twilve and eight-pince tied up in her best apron corner. We 'd as good as a wedding ourselves out of it too; 't was she had the spinding hand, the cr'ature; and we had a roast goose that same night and asked frinds to it. Folks don't have the good fun here they has in the old counthry, sir, so they don't."

"There used to be good times here," said the poor old captain.

"I 'm thinking 't would be a dale the better if you wint and stayed for a while over there," urged the girl affectionately. "It 'll soon be comin' green and illigant while it 's winther here still; the gorse 'll be blooming, sir, and the little daisies thick under your two feet, and you 'd be sitting out in the warm rain and sun, and feeling the good of the ground. If you 'd go to Glengariff, I think you 'd be soon well, I do, then, Captain Balfour, your honor, sir."

"I 'm too old, Nora," replied the captain dismally, but not without interest.

"Sure there ain't a boy in the town that has the spark in his eye like yourself, sir," responded Nora, with encouraging heartiness. "I 'd break away from these sober old folks and the docthers and all, and take ship, and you 'd be soon over the say, and live like a lord in the first cabin; and you 'd land aisy on the tinder in the cove o' Cork, and slape that night in the city, and go next day to the Eccles Hotel in Glengariff. Oh, wisha, the fine place it is wit' the say forninst the garden wall. You 'd get a swim in the clane salt wather, and be as light as a bird.

Sure I would n't be tased wit' so much docthoring and advising, and you none the betther wit' it."

" Why could n't I have a swim in the sea here?" inquired the captain indulgently.

" Sure, it would n't be the same at all," responded Nora, with contempt. " 'T is the sayshore of the old country will do you the most good. The say is very salt entirely by Glengariff; the bay runs up to it, and you 'd get a strong boatman would row you up and down, and you 'd walk in the green lanes, and the folks in the houses would give you good-day ; and if you 'd be afther givin' old Mother Casey a trippence, she 'd down on her two little knees and pray for your honor till you 'd be running home like a light-horseman."

The old man laughed heartily for the first time that day. " I used to be the fastest runner of any lad in school," he said, with pride.

" Sure you might thry it again, wit' Mrs. Casey's kind help, sir," insisted the girl. "Now go to Glengariff this next month o' May, sir, do!"

" Perhaps I will," said the captain decidedly. " I 'm not going to keep up this sort of thing much longer, I can tell them that! If they can't do me any good, they may say so, and I 'll steer my own course. That 's a good idea about the salt water."

The old man fell into a pleasant sleep, with a contented smile on his face. The fire flickered and snapped, and Nora sat still looking into it; her thoughts were far away. Perhaps her unkind aunt would find means to stop the letters between Johnny Morris and herself. Oh, if her mother were only alive, if the scattered household were once more together! It would be a long time at this rate, before she could go back to Johnny with a hundred pounds.

The fire settled itself together and sent up a bright blaze. The old man opened his eyes and looked bewildered; she stepped quickly to his side. "You 'll be askin' for Mr. Reilly?" she said.

"No, no," responded the captain firmly. "What was the name of that place you were talking about?"

"Whiddy Island, sir, where me father was born?" Nora's thoughts had wandered far and wide; she was thinking that she had heard that land was cheap on Whiddy and the fishing fine. She and Johnny had often thought they might do better than in Kenmare.

"No, no," said the captain again, sternly.

"Oh, Glengariff," she exclaimed. "Yes, sir, we were talking "—

"That 's it," responded the captain complacently. "I should like to know something more about the place."

"I was never in it but twice," exclaimed Nora, "but 't was lovely there intirely. My father got work at fishin', and 't was one summer we left Kenmare and went to a place, Baltimore was the name, beyond Glengariff itself, toward the illigant town of Bantry, sir. I saw Bantry, sir, when I was young. We were all alive and together then, my father and mother and all of us; the old shebeen we lived in looked like the skull of a house, it was so old, and the roof falling in on us, but thank God, we were happy in it. Oh, Ireland 's the lovely counthry, sir."

"No bad people at all there ? " asked the captain, looking at her kindly.

"Oh, sir, there are then," said the little maid regretfully. "I have sins upon my own soul, truth I have, sir. The sin of staling was my black shame when I was growing up, then."

"What did you ever steal, child?" asked the captain.

"Mostly eggs, sir," said Nora humbly.

"I dare say you were hungry," said the old man, taking up his newspaper and pretending to frown at the shipping-list.

"Oh, no, captain, 't was not that always. I used to follow an old spickled hen of my mother's and wait for the egg. I 'd track her within the furze, and when I 'd be two days gettin' two eggs I 'd run wit' 'em to sell 'em, and 't was to buy things to sew for me doll I 'd spind the money. I 'd ought to make confission for it now, too. I 'm ashamed, thinkin' of it. And the spickled hen was one that laid very large white eggs intirely, and whiles my poor mother would be missing them, and thinking the old hen was no good and had best be killed, the honest cr'ature, and go to market that way when poulthry was dear. I 'd like one of her eggs now to boil it myself for you, sir; 't would be fine atin' for you coming right in from some place under the green bushes. I think that hen long 's dead, I did n't see her a long while before I was lavin'. A woman called Johanna Spillane bought her from my aunt when my mother was dead. She was a very honest, good hen; a top-knot hen, sir."

"I dare say," said the captain, looking at his newspaper; he did not know why the simple chatter touched and pleased him so. He shrugged his shoulders and moved about in his easy-chair, frowned still more at the shipping-list, and so got the better of his emotion.

"I see that the old brig Miranda has gone ashore on the Florida Keys," he said, as if speaking to a large audience of retired shipmasters. "Stove her bows, rigging cut loose and washed overboard; total wreck. I suppose you never saw a wreck?" He turned and regarded Nora affectionately.

"I did, sir, then," said Nora Connelly, flushing with satisfaction. "We got news of it one morning early, and all trooped to the shore, every grown person and child in the place, laving out Mother Dolan, the ould lady that had no use of her two legs; and all the women, me mother and all, took their babies to her and left them, and she entreatin' — you 'd hear the bawls of her a mile away — that some of the folks would take her wit' 'em on their backs to see what would she get wit' the rest; but we left her screechin' wit' all the poor shilder, and I was there with the first, and the sun coming up,

and the ship breaking up fine out a little
way in the rocks. 'T was loaded with sweet
oranges she was, and they all comin' ashore
like yellow ducklings in the high wather.   I
got me fill for once, I did, indeed."

" Dear, dear," said the captain. "Did the
crew get ashore ? "

" Well, I belave not, sir, but I could n't
rightly say.   I was small, and I took no notice.   I mind there were strangers round
that day, but sailors or the nixt parish was
one to me then. The tide was going out
soon, and then we swarmed aboard, and
wisha, the old ship tipped up wit' us in it,
and I thought I was killed. 'T was a foine
vessel, all gilded round the cabin walls, and
I thought in vain 't would be one like her
comin' to Ameriky.   There was wines
aboard, too, and all the men got their fill.
Mesilf was gatherin' me little petticoat full
of oranges that bobbed in the wather in the
downside of the deck. Wisha, sir, the
min were pushin' me and the other shilder into the wather ; they were very soon
tight, sir, and my own father was wit' 'em,
God rest his soul ! and his cheeks as red
as two roses. Some busybody caught him
ashore and took him to the magistrate, —

that was the squire of our place, sir, and an illigant gentleman. The bliguards was holdin' my father, and I running along, screechin' for fear he 'd be goin' to jail on me. The old squire began to laugh, poor man, when he saw who it was, and says he, 'Is it yoursilf, Davy?' and says my father, 'It 's mesilf, God save your honor, very tight intirely, and feelin' as foine as any lord in Ireland. Lave me go, and I 'll soon slape it off under the next furze-bush that 'll stop still long enough for me by the roadside,' says he. The squire says, 'Lave him go, boys, 't was from his ating the oranges!' says he, and the folks give a great laugh all round. He was doin' no harrum, the poor man! I run away again to the say, then; I forget was there any more happened that day."

"She must have been a fruiter from the Mediterranean. I can't think what she was doing up there on the west coast, out of her bearings," said the captain.

"Faix, sir, I could n't tell you where she was from, if it 's the ship you mane; but she wint no further than our parish and the Black Rocks. I heard tell of plinty other foine wrecks, but I was to that mesilf."

III.

The lengthening days of late winter went slowly by, and at last it was spring, and the windows were left open all day in the captain's room. The household had accepted the fact that nobody pleased the invalid as Nora did, and there was no feeling of jealousy; it was impossible not to be grateful to any one who could invariably spread the oil of sympathy and kindness over such troubled waters. James Reilly and Mrs. Nash often agreed upon the fact that the captain kept all the will he ever had, but little of the good judgment. Yet, in spite of this they took it upon them to argue with him upon every mistaken point. Nora alone had the art of giving a wide berth to dangerous subjects of conversation, and she could twist almost every sort of persistence or aggravation into a clever joke. She had grown very fond of the lonely old man; the instinct toward motherliness in her simple heart was always ready to shelter him from his fancied wrongs, and to quiet him in the darkest hours of fretfulness and pain.

Young Nora Connelly's face had grown

thin during the long winter, and she lost the pretty color from her cheeks as spring came on. She was used to the mild air of Ireland, and to an out-of-door life, and she could not feel like herself in the close rooms of Captain Balfour's house on Barry Street. By the time that the first daffodils were in bloom on the south terrace, she longed inexpressibly for the open air, and used to disappear from even the captain's sight into the garden, where at times she took her turn with the gardeners at spading up the rich soil, and worked with a zeal which put to shame their languid efforts. Something troubled the girl, however; she looked older and less happy; sometimes it was very plain to see that she had been crying.

One morning, when she had been delayed unusually with her downstairs work, the captain grew so impatient that he sent Reilly away to find her. Nora quickly set down a silver candlestick, and wiped her powdery hands upon her apron as she ran upstairs. The captain was standing in the middle of the floor, scowling like a pirate in a picture-book, and even when Nora came in, he did not smile. "I'm going out to take a walk," he said angrily.

"Come on, then, sir," said Nora. "I'll run for your coat and hat, if you'll tell me where" —

"Pooh, pooh, child!"— the pacified captain was smiling broadly. "I only want to take a couple of turns here in the hall. You forget how long I've been house-bound. I'm a good deal better; I'll have that meddling Reilly know it, too; and I won't be told what I may do and what I may not."

"'T is thrue for you, sir," said Nora amiably. "Steady yourself with my arrum, now, and we'll go to the far end of the hall and back again. 'T was the docther himself said a while ago that ye'd ought to thry walking more, and 't was your honor was like to have the life of him. You're a very conthrairy gentleman, if I may be so bold!"

The captain laughed, but the business of dragging his poor heavy foot was more serious than he had expected, in spite of all his brave determination. Nora did her best to beguile him from too much consciousness of his feebleness and disappointment.

"Sure if you'd see ould Mother Killahan come hobbling into church, you'd think yourself as good as a greyhound," she said presently, while the master rested in one of the chairs at the hall's end. " She 's very old intirely. I saw her myself asleep at her beads this morning, but she do be very steady on her two knees, and whiles she prays and says a bead or two, and whiles she gets a bit of sleep, the poor cr'ature. She does be staying in the church a dale this cold weather, and Father Dunn is very aisy with her. She makes the stations every morning of the year, so she does, and one day she come t'rough the deep snow in a great storm there was, and she fell down with weakness on the church steps; and they told Father Dunn, and said how would they get her home, and he come running himself, scolding all the way, and took her up in his arrums, and wint back with her to his own house. You 'd thought she was his own mother, sir. ' She 's one of God's poor,' says he, with the tears in his eyes. Oh, captain, sir! I wish it was Father Dunn was praste to you, I do then! I 'm thinking he 'd know what prayers would be right for you; and himself was born in the country forninst Glengariff, and would tell you how foine it was for your stringth. If you 'd get better, sir, and we 'd meet him on the street, we 'd be afther asking his riverence."

The captain made no answer; he was tired and spent, and sank into his disdained easy-chair, grateful for its comfortable support. The mention of possible help for his feeble frame from any source clung to his erratic memory, and after a few days one of the thoughts that haunted his mind was that Father Dunn, a kind-faced, elderly man, might be of use in this great emergency. To everybody's surprise, his bodily strength seemed to be slowly returning as the spring days went by, but there was oftener and oftener an appealing, childish look in his face,—the firm lines of it were blurred, even while there was a steady renewing of his shattered forces. At last he was able to drive down the busy street one day, with Reilly, in his familiar chaise. The captain's old friends gathered to welcome him, and he responded to their salutations with dignity and evident pleasure; but once or twice, when some one congratulated him upon certain successful matters of business which he had planned before his illness, there was only a troubled look of dullness and almost pain for answer.

One day, Nora Connelly stole out into the garden in the afternoon, and sat there idly

under an old peach-tree. The green fruit
showed itself thick all along the slender
boughs. Nora had been crying already, and
now she looked up through the green leaves
at the far blue sky, and then began to cry
again. She was sadly homesick, poor child!
She longed for her lover, whom she feared
now never to see. Like a picture she re-
called the familiar little group of thatched
houses at home, with their white walls and
the narrow green lanes between ; she saw the
pink daisies underfoot, and the golden gorse
climbing the hill till it stood against the
white clouds. She remembered the figures
of the blue-cloaked women who went and
came, the barefooted, merry children, and the
dabbling ducks ; then she fell to thinking
lovingly of her last walk with Johnny Morris, the empty bird's nest, and all their hopes
and promises the night before she left home.
She had been willful in yielding to her aunt's
plans ; she knew that Johnny feared her
faithlessness, but it was all for love of him
that she had left him. She knew how poor
they were at home. She had faithfully sent
a pound a month to her aunt, and though she
had had angry appeals for more, the other
pound that she could spare, leaving but little

for herself, had been sent in secret to Johnny's mother. She always dreaded the day when her avaricious aunt should find this out and empty all the vials of her wrath of covetousness. Nora, to use her own expression, was as much in dread of this aunt as if the sea were a dry ditch. Alas! she was still the same poor Nora Connelly, though rich and busy America stretched eastward and westward from where she made her new home. It was only by keeping her pounds in her pocket that she could gather enough to be of real and permanent use to those she loved; and yet their every-day woes, real or fictitious, stole the pounds from her one by one.

So she sat crying under the peach-tree until the pale old captain came by, in the box-bordered walk, with scuffling, unsteady steps. He saw Nora and stopped, leaning on his cane.

"Come, come, Nora!" he said anxiously. "What 's the matter, my girl?"

Nora looked up at him and smiled instantly. It was as if the warm Irish sunshine had broken out in the middle of a May shower. A long spray of purple foxglove grew at her feet, and the captain glanced down at it. The sight of it was almost more than she could bear, this flower that grew in the hedgerows at home. She felt as if the flower were exiled like herself and trying to grow in a strange country.

"Don't touch it, sir," she faltered, as the captain moved it with his cane; "'t is very bad luck to meddle with that: they say yourself will be meddled with by the fairies. Fairy Fingers is the name of that flower; we were niver left pick it. Oh, but it minds me of home!"

"What's the matter with you to-day?" asked the captain.

"I've been feeling very sad, sir; I can't help it, either, thinkin' o' me home I've left and me dear lad that I'll see no more. I was wrong to lave him, I was indeed." -

"What lad?" asked Captain Balfour suspiciously. "I'll have no nonsense nor lads about my place. You're too young" — He looked sharply at the tearful young face. "Mrs. Nash can't spare you, either," he added humbly, in a different tone.

"Faix, sir, it's at home he is, in the old counthry, without me; he'll niver throuble ye, me poor Johnny," Nora explained sadly enough. She had risen with proper courtesy, and was standing by the old man; now she ventured to take hold of his arm. He looked flushed and eager, and she forgot herself in the instinct to take care of him.

"Where do you be going so fast?" she asked with a little laugh. "I'm afther believing 't is running away you are."

The captain regarded her solemnly; then he laughed, too. "Come with me," he said. "I'm going to make a call."

"Where would it be?" demanded the girl, with less than her usual deference.

"Come, come! I want to be off," insisted the old gentleman. "We'll go out of this little gate in the fence. I've got to see your Father Dunn on a matter of business," he said, as if he had no idea of accepting any remonstrance.

Nora knew that the doctor and all the elder members of the household approved of her master's amusing himself and taking all the exercise he could. She herself approved his present intentions entirely; it was not for her to battle with the head of the house, at any rate, so she dutifully and with great interest and anxiety set forth beside him down the path, on the alert for any falterings or missteps.

They went out at the gate in the high fence; the master remembered where to find the key, and he seemed in excellent spirits. The side street led them down the hill to Father Dunn's house, but when they reached it the poor captain was tired out. Nora began to be frightened, as she stole a look at him. She had forgotten, in the pride of her own youthful strength, that it would be such a long walk for him. She was anxious about the interview with Father Dunn; she had no idea how to account for their presence, but she had small opinion of the merits and ability of the captain's own parish minister, and felt confident of the good result, in some way, of the visit. Presently the priest's quick step was heard in the passage; Nora rose dutifully as he came in, but was only noticed by a kindly glance. The old captain tried to rise, too, but could not, and Father Dunn and he greeted each other with evident regard and respect. Father Dunn sat down with a questioning look; he was a busy man with a great parish, and almost every one of his visitors came to him with an important errand.

The room was stiff-looking and a little bare; everything in it was well worn. There

was a fine portrait of Father Dunn's predecessor, or, it should rather be said, a poor
portrait of a fine man, whose personal goodness and power of doing Christian service
shone in his face. Father Miles had been
the first priest in that fast-growing inland
town, and the captain had known and respected him. He did not say anything now,
but sat looking up, much pleased, at the
picture. This parlor of the priest's house
had a strangely public and impersonal look;
it had been the scene of many parish weddings and christenings, and sober givings of
rebuke and kindly counsel. Nora gazed
about her with awe; she had been brought
up in great reverence of holy things and of
her spiritual pastors and masters; but she
could not help noticing that the captain was
a little astray in these first few moments.
There stole in upon his pleased contempla-
tion of the portrait a fretful sense of doing
an unaccustomed thing, and he could not regain his familiar dignity and self-possession;
that conscious right to authority which
through long years had stood him in such
good stead. He was only a poor, broken-
down, sick old man; he had never quite
understood the truth about himself before,

and the thought choked him; he could not speak.

"The masther was coveting to spake with your riverence about Glengariff," ventured Nora timidly, feeling at last that the success of the visit depended wholly upon herself.

"Oh, Glengariff, indeed!" exclaimed the good priest, much relieved. He had discovered the pathetic situation at last, and his face grew compassionate.

"This little girl seems to believe that it would set me up to have a change of air. I have n't been very well, Father Dunn." The captain was quite himself again for the moment, as he spoke. "You may not have heard that the doctors have had hold of me lately? Nora, here, has been looking after me very well, and she speaks of some sea-bathing on your Irish coast. I may not be able to leave my business long enough to do any good. It 's going to the dogs, at any rate, but I 've got enough to carry me through."

Nora was flushing with eagerness, but the priest saw how white the old captain's fingers were, where they clasped his walking-stick, how blurred and feeble his face had grown.   The thought of the green hills and hollows along the old familiar shore, the lovely reaches of the bay, the soft air, the flowery hedgerows, came to his mind as if he had been among them but yesterday.

"I wish that you were there, sir, I do indeed," said Father Dunn.   "It is nearer like heaven than any spot in the world to me, is old Glengariff.   You would be pleased there, I 'm certain.   But you 're not strong enough for the voyage, I fear, Captain Balfour.   You 'd best wait a bit and regain your strength a little more.   A man's home is best, I think, when he 's not well."

The captain and Nora both looked defeated.   Father Dunn saw their sadness, and was sure that his kindest duty was to interest this poor guest, and to make a pleasure for him, if possible.

"I can tell you all about it, sir, and how you might get there," he went on hastily, shaking his head to some one who had come to summon him.   " Land at Queenstown, go right up to Cork and pass the night, and then by rail and coach next day, — 't is but a brief journey and you 're there.   'T is a grand little hotel you 'll find close to the bay, — 't was like a palace to me in my boyhood, with the fine tourists coming and going; well, I wish we were there this day, and I showing you up and down the length of the green country."

"Just what I want. I've been a busy man, but when I take a holiday, give me none of your noisy towns," said the captain, eager and cheerful again.

"You'd be so still there that a bird lighting in the thatch would wake you," said Father Dunn. "Ah, 't is many a long year since I saw the place. I dream of it by night sometimes, Captain Balfour, God bless it!"

Nora could not keep back the ready tears. The very thought that his reverence had grown to manhood in her own dear country-side was too much for her.

"You 're not thinking of going over this summer?" asked the captain wistfully. "I should be gratified if you would bear me company, sir; I 'd try to do my part to make it pleasant." But the good father shook his head and rose hastily, to stand by the window that looked out into his little garden.

"We 'd make a good company," said he presently, turning toward them and smiling, "with young Nora here to show us our way.

You can't have had time yet, my child, to forget the old roads across country!" and Nora fairly sobbed.

"Pray for the likes of-me, sir!" she faltered, and covered her face with her hands. "Oh, pray for the masther too, your riverence Father Dunn, sir; 'tis very wake he is, and 'tis mesilf that's very lonesome in Ameriky, an' I'm afther laving the one I love!"

"Be quiet, now!" said the priest gravely, checking her with a kindly touch of his hand, and glancing at Captain Balfour. The poor old man looked in a worried way from one to the other, and Father Dunn went away to fetch him a glass of wine. Then he was ready to go home, and Father Dunn got his hat and big cane, pleading that an errand was taking him in the same direction.

"If I thought it would do me any good, I would start for that place we were speaking of to-morrow," said the captain as they set forth. "You know to what I refer, the sea-bathing and all." The priest walked slowly; the captain's steps grew more and more faltering and unsteady. Nora Connelly followed anxiously. There flitted through Father Dunn's mind phrases out of the old

Bible story,— "a great man and honorable;" "a valiant man and rich," "but a leper;" the little captive maid that brought him to the man of God. Alas, Father Dunn could tell the captain of no waters of Jordan that would make him a sound man; he could only say to him, "Go in peace," like the prophet of old.

When they reached home the household already sought the captain in despair, but it happened that nobody was in the wide, cool hall as they entered.

"I hope that you will come in and take a glass of wine with me. You have treated me with brotherly kindness, sir," said the master of the house; but Father Dunn shook his head and smiled as he made the old man comfortable in a corner of the broad sofa, taking his hat and stick from him and giving them to Nora. "Not to-day, Captain Balfour, if you will excuse me."

The captain looked disappointed and childish. "I am going to send you a bottle of my father's best old madeira," he said. "Sometimes, when a man is tired out or has a friend come in to dine"— But he was too weary himself to finish the sentence. The old house was very still; there were distant

voices in the garden; a door at the end of
the hall opened into an arbor where flickers
of light were shining through the green vine
leaves. Everything was stately and handsome; there was a touch everywhere of that
colonial elegance of the captain's grandfather's time which had never been sacrificed
to the demon of change, that restless American spirit which has spoiled the beauty of
so many fine and simple old houses.

The priest was used to seeing a different
sort of household interior, his work was
among the poor. Then he looked again at
the house's owner, an old man, sick, sorry,
and alone. "God bless you, sir," he said.
"I must be going now."

"Come and see me again," said the captain, opening his eyes. "You are a good
man; I am glad to have your blessing." The
words were spoken with a manly simplicity
and directness that had always been liked
by Captain Balfour's friends. "Nora," he
whispered, when Father Dunn had gone,
"we'll say nothing to Mrs. Nash. I must
rest a little while here before we get up the
stairs."

IV.

Toward the end of the summer, things had grown steadily worse, and Captain Balfour was known to be failing fast. The clerks had ceased to come for his signature long before; he had forgotten all about business and pleasure too, and slept a good deal, and sometimes was glad to see his friends and sometimes indifferent to their presence. But one day, when he felt well enough to sit in his great chair by the window, he told Mr. Barton, his good friend and lawyer, that he wished to attend to a small matter of business. "I 've arranged everything long ago, as an aging man should," he said. "I don't know that there 's any hurry, but I 'll mention this item while I think of it. Nora, you may go downstairs," he said sharply to the girl, who had just entered upon an errand of luncheon or medicine, and Nora disappeared; she remembered afterward that it was the only time when, of his own accord and seeming impatience, he had sent her away.

Reilly and Mrs. Nash bore no ill-will toward their young housemate; they were reasonable enough to regard Captain Balfour's fondness for her with approval. There was something so devoted and single-hearted about the young Irish girl that they had become fond of her themselves. They had their own plans for the future, and looked forward to being married when the captain should have no more need of them. It really hurt Mrs. Nash's feelings when she often found Nora in tears, for the desperate longing for home and for Johnny Morris grew worse in the child's affectionate heart instead of better.

One day Reilly had gone down town, leaving the captain asleep. Nora was on guard; Mrs. Nash was at hand in the next room with her sewing, and Nora sat still by the window; the captain was apt to sleep long and heavily at this time of the day. She was busy with some crocheting; it was some edging of a pattern that the sisters of Kenmare had taught Johnny Morris's mother. She gave a little sigh at last and folded her hands in her lap; her gray Irish eyes were blinded with tears.

"What's the matter, child?" asked the captain unexpectedly; his voice sounded very feeble.

Nora started; she had forgotten him and his house.

" Will you have anything, sir ? " she asked anxiously.

" No, no ; what 's the matter, child ? " asked the old man kindly.

" 'T is me old story ; I 'm longing for me home, and I can't help it if I died too. I 'm like a thing torn up by the roots and left in the road. You 're very good, sir, and I would never lave the house and you in it, but 't is home I think of by night and by day ; how ever will I get home ? "

Captain Balfour looked at her compassionately. " You 're a good girl, Nora ; perhaps you 'll go home before long," he said.

" 'T is sorra a few goes back ; Ameriky 's the same as heaven for the like o' that," answered Nora, trying to smile, and drying her eyes. " There 's many 'd go back too but for the presents every one looks to have ; 't would take a dale of money to plase the whole road as you pass by. 'T is a kind of fever the young ones has to be laving home. Some laves good steady work and home and friends, that might do well. There 's getting to be fine chances for smart ones there with so many laving."

" Yes, yes," said the captain ; " we 'll talk that over another time, I want to go to sleep now;" and Nora flushed with shame and took up her crocheting again. " 'T was me hope of growing rich, and me aunt's tongue shaming me that gets the blame," she murmured to herself. The sick man's hands looked very white and thin on the sides of his chair; she looked at them and at his face, and her heart smote her for selfishness. She was glad to be in America, after all.

They never said anything to each other now about going to Glengariff; a good many days slipped by when the captain hardly spoke except to answer questions; but in restless evenings, when he could not sleep, people who passed by in the street could hear Nora singing her old familiar songs of love and war, sometimes in monotonous, plaintive cadences that repeated and repeated a refrain, sometimes in livelier measure, with strange thrilling catches and prolonged high notes, as a bird might sing to its mate in the early dawn out in the wild green pastures. The lovely weird songs of the ancient Irish folk, how old they are, how sweet they are, who can tell? but now and then a listener of the new world of the western seas hears them with deep delight, hears them with a strange, golden sense of dim remembrance, a true, far-descended birthright of remembrance that can only come from inheritance of Celtic blood.

When the frost had fallen on the old garden, Captain Balfour died, and his year of trouble was ended. Reilly and Mrs. Nash, the cook and Nora, cried bitterly in the kitchen, where the sudden news found them. Nobody could wish him to come back, but they cried the more when they thought of that. There was a great deal said about him in the newspapers; about his usefulness in town and State, his wealth, his character, and his history; but nobody knew so well as this faithful household how comfortable he had made his lonely home for other people; and those who knew him best thought most of his kindness, his simple manliness, and sincerity of word and deed.

The evening after the funeral, Nora was all alone in her little room under the high roof. She sat on the broad seat of a dormer window, where she could look far out over the city roofs to a glimpse of the country beyond. There was a new moon in the sky, the sunset was clear, the early autumn weather was growing warm again.

The old house was to belong to a nephew of the captain, his only near relative, who had spent a great many years abroad with an invalid wife; it was to be closed for the present, and Mrs. Nash and Mr. Reilly were to be married and live there all winter, and then go up country to live in the spring, where Mrs. Nash owned a little farm. She was of north of Ireland birth, was Mrs. Nash; her first husband had been an American. She told Nora again and again that she might always have a home with her, but the fact remained that Nora must find herself a new place, and she sat in the window wondering with a heavy heart what was going to happen to her. All the way to the burying-ground and back again in the carriage, with the rest of the household, she had sobbed and mourned, but she cried for herself as much as for the captain. Poor little Irish Nora, with her warm heart and her quick instincts and sympathies! how sadly she thought now of the old talk about going to Glengariff; she had clung long to her vain hope that the dream would come true, and that the old captain and his household were all going over seas together, and so she should get home. Would anybody in America ever be so kind again and need her so much as the captain?

Some one had come to the foot of the stairs and was calling Nora loudly again and again. It was dark in the upper entryway, however bright the west had looked just now from her window. She left her little room in confusion; she had begun already to look over her bits of things, her few clothes and treasures, before she packed them to go away. Mrs. Nash seemed to be in a most important hurry, and said that they were both wanted in the dining-room, and it was very pleasant somehow to be wanted and made of consequence again. She had begun to feel like such an unnecessary, stray little person in the house.

The lamps were lighted in the handsome old dining-room, it was orderly and sedate; one who knew the room half expected to see Captain Balfour's fine figure appear in the doorway to join the waiting group. There were some dark portraits on the wall, and the old Balfour silver stood on the long sideboard. Mrs. Nash had set out all the best furnishings, for this day when the master of the house left it forever.

There were not many persons present, and

Nora sat down, as some one bade her, feeling very disrespectful as she did it.   Mr. Barton, the lawyer, began to read slowly from a large folded paper; it dawned presently upon Nora that this was the poor captain's will.   There was a long bequest to the next of kin, there were public gifts, and gifts to different friends, and handsome legacies to faithful Mrs. Nash and James Reilly, and presently the reading was over.   There was something quite grand in listening to this talk of thousands and estates, but little Nora, who had no call, as she told herself, to look for anything, felt the more lonely and friendless as she listened.   There was a murmur of respectful comment as the reading ended, but Mr. Barton was opening another paper, a small sheet, and looked about him, expecting further attention.

"I am sure that no one will object to the carrying out of our deceased friend's wishes as affirmed in this more recent memorandum. Captain Balfour was already infirm at the time when he gave me the directions, but, as far as I could judge, entirely clear in his mind.   He dictated to me the following bequest and signed it.   The signature is, I own, nearly illegible, but I am sure that, under the somewhat affecting circumstances, there will be no opposition."

"I desire" (read Mr. Barton slowly),—"I desire the executors of my will to pay five hundred dollars within one month after my death to Nora Connelly; also, to secure her comfortable second-class passage to the port of Queenstown, in Ireland. I mean that, if she still desires, she may return to her home. I am sensible of her patience and kindness, and I attempt in this poor way to express my gratitude to a good girl. I wish her a safe return, and that every happiness may attend her future life.

"JOHN BALFOUR."

" 'T is a hundred pounds for ye an' yer passage, me darlin'," whispered the cook excitedly. " 'T is mesilf knew you would n't be forgotten an' the rist of us so well re-mimbered. 'T is foine luck for ye ; Heaven rist his soul, the poor captain ! "

Nora was sitting pale and silent. She did not cry now; her heart was deeply touched, her thoughts flew homeward. She seemed to hear the white waves breaking about the ship, and to see the far deep colors of the Irish shore. For Johnny had said again and again that if they had a hundred pounds and their two pairs of hands, he could do as well with his little farm as any man in Ireland.

" Sind for your lad to come over," urged Cousin Donahue, a day later, when the news had been told ; but Nora proudly shook her head. She had asked for her passage the very next week. It was a fine country, America, for those with the courage for it, but not for Nora Connelly, that had left her heart behind her. Cousin Donahue laughed and shook his head at such folly, and offered a week's free lodging to herself and Johnny the next spring, when she 'd be the second time a greenhorn coming over. But Nora laughed too, and sailed away one Saturday morning in late October, across the windy sea to Ireland.

V.

Again it was gray twilight after a short autumn day in the old country, and a tall Irish lad was walking along the high-road that led into Kenmare. He was strong and eager for work, but his young heart was heavy within him. The piece of land which he held needed two men's labor, and work as he might, he must fall behind with his rent.

It was three years since that had happened before, and he had tried so hard to do well with his crops, and had even painfully read a book that was wise about crops which the agent had lent him, and talked much besides with all the good farmers. It was no use, he could not hold his own; times were bad and sorrowful, and Nora was away. He had believed that, whatever happened to her fortunes, he should be able in time to send for her himself and be a well-off man. Oh, for a hundred pounds in his pocket to renew his wornout land! to pay a man to help him with the new ditching. Oh, for courage to fight his way to independence on Irish ground! "I've only got my heart and my two hands, God forgive me!" said Johnny Morris aloud. "God be good to me and Norry, and me poor mother! May be I'll be after getting a letter from me darling the night; 't is long since she wrote."

He stepped back among the bushes to let a side-car pass that had come up suddenly behind him. He recognized the step of Dinny Killoren's fast pacer, and looked to see if there were room on the car for another passenger, or if perhaps Dinny might be alone and glad to have company. There was only Dinny himself and a woman, who gave a strange cry. The pacer stopped, and Johnny's heart beat within him as if it would come out of his breast. "My God, who's this?" he said.

"Lift me down, lift me down!" said the girl. "Oh, God be thanked, I'm here!" And Johnny leaped forward and caught Nora Connelly in his arms.

"Is it yoursilf?" he faltered, and Nora said, "It's mesilf indeed, then." Dinny Killoren laughed aloud on the side-car, with his pacer backing and jumping and threatening to upset all Nora's goods in the road. There was a house near by; a whiff of turf smoke, drifting low in the damp air, blew into Nora's face; she heard ‚the bells begin to ring in Kenmare. It was the evening of a saint's day, and they rang and rang, and Nora had come home.

So she married the lad she loved, and was a kind daughter to his mother. They spent a good bit of the captain's money on their farm, and gave it a fine start, and were able to flaunt their prosperity in the face of that unkind aunt who had wished to make them spend their lives apart. They were seen early on market days in Kenmare, and Nora only laughed when foolish young people said that the only decent country in the world was America. Sometimes she sat in her doorway in the long summer evening and thought affectionately of Captain Balfour, the poor, kind gentleman, and blessed herself devoutly. Often she said a prayer for him on Sunday morning as she knelt in the parish church, with flocks of blackbirds singing outside among the green hedges, under the lovely Irish sky.